a martyr for
suzy kosasovich

PATRICK MICHAEL FINN

a martyr for suzy kosasovich

Winner of the Ruthanne Wiley Memorial
Novella Contest, as selected by Tom Barbash

Cleveland State University Poetry Center
Cleveland, Ohio
IMAGINATION SERIES #15

Cleveland State University Poetry Center, Cleveland, Ohio
Printed in the United States of America
Printed on acid free paper

LCCN 2007051700
ISBN 978-1-880834-77-0

This book is a winner of the Ruthanne Wiley
Memorial Novella Contest, selected by Tom Barbach,
and is a title in the **imagination** series published
by the Cleveland State University Poetry Center,
2121 Euclid Avenue, Cleveland OH 44115-2214.

Book design by BookMatters, Berkeley
Set in Dante
Cover design by Frank Cucciarre, Blink Concept
Cover photo by Richard Younker
Author photo by Valerie Bandura
Printed and bound at CSS Publishing Company, Lima, Ohio

Library of Congress Cataloging-in-Publication Data

Finn, Patrick Michael, 1973–
    A martyr for Suzy Kosasovich / Patrick Michael Finn.
        p.   cm. — (**imagination** series ; #15)
    ISBN 978-1-880834-77-0 (alk. paper)
    1. Teenage girls—Fiction. 2. Rape—Fiction. 3. Working
class—Fiction. 4. Joliet (Ill.)—Fiction. 5. Domestic fiction.
I. Title.
PS3606.I559M39   2008
813'.6—dc22   2007051700

for my family:
Mom, Dad, Katie, and Danny

a martyr for
suzy kosasovich

After her parents left for their Friday night bowling league, Suzy Kosasovich helped Busha clear what was left of the red cabbage and fish from the kitchen table. They put the dishes in the sink, then filled it with water to let them soak. The old woman patted her granddaughter on the cheek and called her My Good Angel and said, "And now we go to the Stations." They put on their sweaters and walked down the stoop to the cracked, crooked sidewalk that led to Saint Cyril's for Stations of the Cross, the service that took place every Friday night during Lent.

Busha had moved in many months before, right after Dzia Dzia had died. Suzy didn't really mind taking her to church; she was still a year or two too young to need Friday nights of freedom with friends. But she knew that soon these nights would mean much to her, just as these nights meant much to the other young she saw driving around in packed cars, smoking cigarettes and tongue-kissing. She was looking forward to nights like that. Sacks of beer and wine under the black train bridge this side of the barge canal wall. The barges, loaded with fuel, coal, garbage, and rebar, would slowly troll past, sometimes so close to the canal wall that the kids would pitch empty bottles at them to see the dust of glass explode on impact, the broken bits shimmering in the moonlight and falling into the waterway, rippling the oil-slick, silver-black surface before it folded and turned in the trolling scow's wake. And summers of naked night-swimming in the abandoned rock pits that pocked the southern edge of town. Then making out in somebody's dark bedroom above a big party in some far-off nice big city she might even move to when she was old enough to leave home.

"Can you smell the trees?" Busha said.

During most of Lent's forty days, the trunks of the bare trees that lined Pulaski Street were speckled white with street salt, and the only sounds in the neighborhood at night were the occasional church bells calling the Angelus and Hours, and then the heavy iron thrum of engines and shrieking shift whistles from Joliet Washer and Wire, the rusty old plant on the barge canal just a few blocks down the hill.

But now Lent was almost over. Branches were thickening with buds, and it was warm enough for the Zimne Piwo Club on the corner to have its front doors propped open. Now moths instead of snowflakes circled in the blue band of light on the Old Style sign that hung above the entrance. Jukebox polkas and shouts bounced onto the street and drowned out the hard ugly sounds from the plant. The horns and accordions from a corny old Joliet Jugoslavs record blared from inside. The sudden roar of music and noisy laughter inspired Suzy to imagine whispered invitations to long rides in cars packed with friends who all wanted her along for the secret trip to the big rich party in the city. She would always make them laugh and blush. They would share their beer and hold her hand and tell her they loved having her along.

But Busha shook her head and covered her ears as they passed the tavern doors. "Bah, Lord, drunks," she said.

Suzy stopped and glanced inside. She wasn't allowed to go in,

4

but suddenly she wanted to, and badly. She saw the crowd of men from her neighborhood, still in greasy plant clothes with their caps crammed into their back pockets, some in damp undershirts, drinking tap Old Style while they watched the White Sox night game on the black-and-white set that hung on the wall behind the bar where the owner, Fat Kuputzniak, served shots and drenched glasses of pale yellow beer as fast as the men drank them. And the men always drank their shots and taps as fast as they could, until the long week was numbed from their shoulders, and they slumped on the bar in the waking daze of booze.

Then, for the first time in many months, she saw Mickey Grogan, too young to be inside but pink and drunk nonetheless, an old grade school classmate who squinted at her, swaying, through the smoke, waving like an idiot. She pretended not to notice him, and when he kept waving she was afraid he might call out to her. He eventually shrugged and turned back to his drink.

Busha had gone many steps ahead before she realized Suzy wasn't next to her. She turned around and said, "Angel, come on," but Suzy didn't hear her.

Mickey Grogan was a few years older than Suzy, but he'd always been held back in school grade after grade until he finally dropped out, a sophomore at seventeen, and went to work at the plant. Mickey had always waved whenever he saw Suzy on the street. She liked the idea of an older boy paying attention to her, even if he was a dropout who'd be stuck at the plant forever. No one else seemed to notice her.

One night the summer before, Mickey took his waving a step further by crossing the street to see her. They ended up going for a walk. He'd been to the Zimne Piwo Club, and he was very drunk, but Suzy let him put his arm around her in a way that seemed harmless given the things he wanted to talk about: memories of the fat nuns from grade school, the parakeets he kept, his mother's pickle loaf, the way his foreman, Jenko, farted all over the plant. It felt like talking to somebody's uncle. She had been charmed. But with his arm around her she was close enough to smell the odors in his mouth, not just booze, but a rot, and to notice that he was already missing one of his blunt yellow teeth. She tried to tell him that she had to get home, but he wouldn't listen, and finally he laughed and stopped walking and said, "Goddamn, you're really pretty lovely, Suzy, you know?" then clutched at one of her breasts and tried to push his tongue into her mouth. She pushed him away and marched, and he trailed behind her, blubbering about how sorry he was. When she looked back, she saw that he was dramatically kneeling on the sidewalk and weeping into his hands like a neglected lover from a movie. She was angrily embarrassed for him, then sickened for herself. The slick of his spittle on her lips tasted like filthy liquor. And that rot. Maybe it was pus. Maybe his gums had a disease that made pus seep out at the gum line. She spat, still walking, with her arms squeezed against her. When she got home and ran up the front stoop, she could still hear him sobbing her name all the way from the spot where she'd left him. She decided for a while that she'd never again let any boy get that close to her.

She had not seen Mickey Grogan since. Now here he was, thin as a bum, with wet red hair hanging past his eyes, sloppy so early in a dim noisy bar and grinning like an infant, and Suzy was heavily reminded of not only that night with him, but of what her own Friday nights with friends and booze and boys might turn into.

"Come on," Busha said, pulling on her arm. "All it takes is a minute and you'll smell like that place, bah."

In Saint Cyril's they sat among the other women who went to Stations every Friday night, women who wore dark coats and head scarves, who fingered their rosaries and murmured novenas and lined up after every service to kiss the jeweled icon to the Black Virgin of Czestochowa.

The service began, Father Zajc and two altar boys stopping below each of the fourteen Stations of the Cross and praying, *We adore You, Oh Christ, and we praise You, because by Your Holy Cross You have redeemed the world,* and as the old women murmured a drone of response that barely made an echo, Suzy Kosasovich was quickly lost into her own boredom. She looked around at the stained glass windows, always black and colorless at night. She saw the saints that lined the walls of the church, her imagination still in the music and smoke from the Zimne Piwo Club, and still the promise and panic about her own Friday nights that the music and smoke and drunk Mickey Grogan had given her. There were saints painted way up in the white dome high above the altar, their arms outstretched in heavenly glory among the fluttering baby angels, and she wondered about how someone could get up that high to paint all that, the flowing robes and dainty wings. The other saints were statues on smaller side altars all along the church, with sad eyes that stared down at the flowers and candles along their plaster feet, and the Virgin Mary's feet stepping on a wild snake with fangs in his wide twisted mouth. She had seen these church things hundreds of times, but she was getting so sick of having to sit there that she couldn't think of anything else to do but look around at them, maybe watch for one of their eyes to move and open wide like a horror movie possession. She scared herself and looked away, taking up and thumbing through one of the missals piled at both ends of the pew.

Some of the saints were martyrs, Suzy knew. They were saints who had been beaten, stoned, raped, scalded, pierced with arrows, gouged, hung on crosses upside down, their final moments dripping with unimaginable agonies just like Christ's, worse than

7

Christ's, all for the glorious, forbidden pride of their faith in Him. These concepts escaped Suzy's limited senses of faith and empathy. They were just random holy stories she remembered vaguely from catechism classes. She thought about them rarely, and only in a guilty, protective allegiance to Busha whenever she happened to talk about them, their legendary tortures, Glory to Christ, on feast days and after high masses of obligation.

After the last Station, the Eucharistic bells rang for Benediction and Father Zajc raised the rounded golden monstrance wrapped in silk with both hands above the altar, the white disc of host behind a circle of glass in the middle of the radiantly holy gold, a bursting halo of rich light around an empty eye blinded by the flash of God, raised high three times and shining above the ringing bells, and above the *ting ting ting* of the silver sensor chain the altar boy swung on his knees at the bottom of the altar, the white spiced incense smoldering and climbing. The old women were singing *Pange Lingua Gloriosi. Sing, My Tongue, the Savior's Glory.* There was no organ or choir to lead them, and they sounded shaky and awful, like sick children, singing from their thin, wet, wrinkled throats. Suzy soon stopped following the mysteries and rites of the service entirely and drifted into an imaginative comparison between the martyrs who lined the church and the suffering who lived, still-living, right outside in the narrow houses along Pulaski Street, the still-living martyrs who weren't painted high in the dome or sculpted standing sadly with flowers and candles at their feet, and who weren't suffering for anything bigger than Pulaski Street itself. She imagined the dome above the altar grandly painted with the pregnant young who grew fat, battered, and stretched with too many children, stuffed into cheap white jeans and sneakers, functioning just to serve an ugly husband who came home from work griping about his foreman and gripping his big purple thing in his fist. Then she imagined statues for those same ugly husbands who suffered to keep Joliet Washer and Wire running with their hammers and wrenches and oil-stained clothes, stupidly stuck to those machines forever (like they'd never heard of anything else to do, of anywhere else in the world to go but crummy Joliet) and whining about it over their Zimne Piwo Club beer and booze that worked to briefly lift them from the fact that they'd all have to go back the next day. Then a statue for Fat Kuputzniak, who suffered to keep the Zimne Piwo Club standing with his bottomless kegs and bottles, bearing in pious presentation a rag and a glass instead of a cross with flowers. And then a special altar for Mickey Grogan, patron martyr of Pulaski Street's many young disasters who, not yet twenty, trembled in withdrawal from drink and dropped rotten teeth, a bloodshot statue sculpted with a stupid wave and a rotten mouth and, tenderly open and loose at his side, relaxed fingers ready to grasp each passing breast. Suzy Kosasovich wanted to laugh at how stupid a church like that would look, until she imagined what her own statue might look like: Saint Suzy Kosasovich of Fast Friday Night Liquor, flat on her back with a black eye and a split lip, legs spread below hiked, saintly garments, a shrine where lonely men would rub out staggered offerings of sperm in the wavy candlelit dark of the empty church late at night after the bars had closed and everyone had gone home, leaving Saint Cyril's the only place open at that hour for Perpetual Adoration. She squeezed her eyes closed and said to herself, *Jesus Jesus Jesus*, understanding that once she hit her own Friday nights, whenever that would happen, knowing it would be sooner or never, there wouldn't be anyone but herself to protect her from the consequences of things that every child wants and needs to try.

"You didn't pray," Busha said as they were walking home.

Suzy denied it, promised nothing was wrong, the lie roaring

from inside where her secret progression into the chaos of maturity had already started, burning her far beyond the pain that sometimes came before the rush of her monthly bleeding.

Busha stopped her and said, "Here. Take this," holding out to Suzy what looked like a coin on the end of a chain. "It's a relic," Busha said. "A relic to Saint Rufina. You wear it. You pray to her and you'll be all right in this place."

Busha kept hundreds of religious items—relics, holy cards, medals, rosaries—and she had given many to Suzy, so many that they carried little significance anymore beyond a grandmother's gesture of kindness. But tonight this relic was a part of the new terrors Suzy wanted to keep to herself, and especially from Busha. She had to force herself to take and look at the relic. It was flat, flower-shaped, about the size of a quarter. There was a circle of glass in the center, and inside was a gray ragged swatch of something planted above the words *Saint Rufina Pray For Us.*

"There in the middle," Busha said. "That's a piece of her garments. Saint Rufina's garments. It's holy. Blessed."

Suzy put the chain around her neck and let the relic drop into her shirt. The metal chilled the skin between her breasts.

"Thank you," she said.

When they passed the Zimne Piwo Club, the doors were closed and the racket and music inside were muffled. But Suzy heard a distinct and crazed laugh inside that, she was certain, belonged to Mickey Grogan.

She was right. The doors flew open behind them and a few sodden men loudly stumbled onto Pulaski Street. Mickey Grogan was with them, his wet red hair hanging over his face, his cackling laugh a piercing echo in the night. He didn't see Suzy and Busha because they had already turned into the streetlight branch shadows for home.

Then one of the men got sick on the street with a great gush of hacking and splash that made the others moan and laugh.

"There goes the Cigarette King," Mickey Grogan said. "There he goes, boys. The Pussy King of Pulaski Street."

Busha shook her head and, in the old language, whispered, "Lord preserve us from those dangers closest to us."

There had been lots of talk from the older kids on the bus about Good Friday, the first day off school for Easter vacation, the day most fathers took additional shifts at the plant for the union holiday triple pay, and most mothers, extra hours at their various jobs for Easter basket money, and the day Fat Kuputzniak each year drank himself into a jostled, tottering bucket of phlegm and opened up the Zimne Piwo Club beer and booze to anyone with a wallet.

A bum age fate that year had cast Suzy Kosasovich as the only ninth grader to ride the 502 Lidice route to and from Joliet West High School each day, so she always took the bus by herself. But she always listened, always heard things, had heard that Fat Kuputzniak's younger sister had been hit by a car and killed one Good Friday many years before, which was why he got so drunk, why he didn't check any ID's, and why he had once served an eight-year-old who couldn't even see over the bar. It had nothing to do with a sorrowful commemoration of Jesus Christ's death, and the older kids on the bus couldn't wait. They were going to get plastered and tear the fuckin' place to shit worse than any other year.

And now Good Friday was only a few weeks away, and Suzy, listening to the older kids on the bus without even a glance from any of them, was thinking about going to the Zimne Piwo Club by herself on Good Friday and drinking beer among them. Did she really need an invitation to do something like that? It was a public place on a public street, and they all might get a kick out of seeing her, Suzy Kosasovich, the youngest and quietest on board—did they even know her name?—just walk up to the bar and tell Fat Kuputzniak she wanted a beer. She knew that the older kids on the bus never paid any attention to her, but this didn't bother her too much. She was still young, and besides, she was actually afraid of them, guys and girls alike, their tattered jean jackets patched with the skulls, snakes, and swords of their favorite metal bands, their shades, their painted lips, eyes, nails, and huge frosted curls, dirty boots, hot pink gum, their shouting, laughing, hitting, and sexy kissing. Especially Darly Shapinka and Joey Korosa, who were usually cloudy-eyed and cool, the toughest, unless Joey brought a bag of wine on board, sometimes pills, and then they'd tongue kiss each other, or argue, and Darly would get loud and brag about how she was going to do him hot and good when they got home, and that if any other bitch even looked at Joey she'd kick her fuckin' ass, all the guys laughing and the girls looking away from fear, and Joey would tell her to shut up, he wasn't her boyfriend, he wasn't anybody's goddamn boy-friend, and then Darly would get upset and go cry by herself in the back. But usually they were quiet, pissed off, mumbling to each other, holding hands off and on. Nobody messed with them.

Darly had skinny legs and arms, but her belly and bottom were thick and her breasts hung huge, which worked to explain the ru-mors that she'd already had two kids (*by a nigger,* they all said) and had given them away to the Holy Ghost Fathers Orphanage over in Chicago Heights. But Suzy didn't think Darly was ugly. Her teeth were good, and she kept her hair pulled back in a tight, gel-slicked tail—the way bad girls always did when they wanted to fight, and Darly Shapinka always did. So did Joey. His nose bad been busted from fighting, and it bent sharply from his face in a way that made him look older and exotic, both of which he actually was. He had been an athlete in football, but he'd gotten kicked off the team for failing all his classes and his piss test for cocaine. *Cocaine.* Aside from people on television and in movies, Suzy had never known *anyone* who'd tried cocaine. Among the glue-sniffers, pill-poppers, boozers, and pot-heads who roamed the yellow and brown locker-lined hallways of Joliet West High School, cocaine seemed as elegant and as foreign as the California coastline itself.

Joey and Darly were both nineteen, both second-chance twelfth graders trying to make up the time and grades lost from countless months of ditching school, failed classes, long-term suspensions, and appealed expulsions for Fighting, Drug Possession, Minor Property Destruction, and General Disrespect and Defiance of Authority, all of which were clearly defined in Joliet West High School's Standards of Academic Conduct and was passed out in flimsily stapled mimeographed booklets at the beginning of each year during the Mandatory Schoolwide Orientation Assembly held in the Anton Bradeska Memorial Gymnasium. The students would clobber up into the rafters and slouch through the presentations concerning their futures, their success, and the importance of a high school education. The students would rip farts and laugh and piss and moan about the stupid goddamn rules and the stupid goddamn school, Christ, what a load of shit it was to have to come back and deal with all the asshole teachers. Eventually some students would yank pages out of their booklets and roll them into enormous comedy joints that were twisted at the ends and passed around from row to howling row, until the teachers confiscated them and chastised and wrote Discipline Referrals that, everybody knew, would get filed in a folder somewhere and forgotten. But most of the students crumpled the booklets up and ditched them in the garbage cans or right on the floor on their way out of the gymnasium, knowing that murder itself was the only infraction that could actually get you kicked out of Joliet West High School for good. Suzy still had her copy of the Standards of Academic Conduct tucked neatly in the front pocket of her assignment binder that she carried from class to class, then home in her backpack. She never needed to look at it because she was never in danger of doing anything wrong.

Somebody on the bus had recently asked Joey Korosa if he was finally going to finish school this year. "Goddamn right I am," Joey answered. And when asked about what he planned on doing after graduation, Joey said, "Drink, fuck, and fight. In that order. Until they lock me up for good." He and Darly had been drinking wine again, and she laughed her sooty grown-up laugh and added, "You can do *me* drunk, honey. And fight any fucker who gives you any bullshit."

Nobody challenged these claims, and nothing else was added. What could have been said that wouldn't have provoked a threat, more yelling, and finally an attack? Suzy wasn't the only person who was afraid of Joey Korosa and Darly Shapinka. Everyone on that bus was afraid of them, and the older people and old people who rode that route to work would make sour faces and shake their heads whenever Joey and Darly openly drank and made out. One time a fat froggish woman in big plastic purple glasses stood up and admonished them for their lack of respect, their ugly behavior, and their filthy language before she righteously exited the bus several stops too early in an act of transportational protest that left the students laughing, mocking her anger by repeating what she said in twisted falsettos that were halted when Darly spat on the floor and said, "That bitch better mind her own fuckin' business and if she wants to ride this bus she better just keep her mouth shut and deal with it or else I'm gonna make her take back her words and make her fuckin' eat them."

And where others channeled their fears of Joey and Darly into disdain, hatred, or sugary deference, Suzy was instead fascinated by their carelessness. Sure, Darly was dirty and loose, but she wore it with a cool dignity that Suzy sort of admired, a girl who was bad enough to act in ways that brought her stained reputations she didn't care about.

She imagined Friday and Saturday nights with a girl like Darly Shapinka, who would take her in and show her the mysteries of basements and vacant parks where she and her friends would get drunk and high and give head to the thick-armed and long-haired guys who tore through town in black Chevys blasting Black Sabbath. She wondered what it would be like to be noticed in school and on the bus as one of Darly and Joey's friends. She would be proud, cool, pissed off, talked about. Feared. Then she would be closer to Joey, older, exotic Joey, whose drink-fight-and-fuck gradu-ation plan was, as far as Suzy could see, simply an act to uphold his own reckless reputation. How could somebody who looked like that, who looked so much older and more mature, someone who carried himself with such a distant calm really plan on pissing his life away like the rest of the people on the bus? Suzy didn't believe it. She saw in Joey Korosa a beautifully jagged young man who would someday leave like she would and stretch himself out to a bigger, richer place where his dangerous past would serve to build his promise among the sheltered and inexperienced who would gasp in awe of whatever he would accomplish. Maybe he'd be an artist in Chicago, a rough, gorgeous painter who slopped out works of art in his own studio loft downtown that was packed with the paintings he'd casually show to her when they were alone. He would point to their features with the two fingers he held his ciga-rettes with, pausing to take long drags and explain their purpose and meaning in cool instruction that would travel from his nose and mouth in easy white puffs or artistic smoke. Maybe she'd be an artist in the city like that too. She'd already taken drawing classes at the high school, and her teachers told her she had talent, drive, and vision when it came to her fuzzy, penciled renderings of cut-out fashion magazine models.

Which is why Suzy didn't feel too sorry for herself when the older kids on the bus, especially Darly and Joey, didn't see her; she had never once offered herself to be seen. But someday Joey and Darly would find her a younger daring equal, would find her when the right moment came to prove that she was much different from and tougher than all the others, who only knew how to frightfully kiss their asses. What if she got kicked off the bus for telling some nosey old woman to go fuck herself? Or boarded with a smoke hanging from her mouth? The driver would tell her to put it the hell out, smoking ain't allowed, and she'd flick that butt right at his fat face. He'd gasp, and when he tried to get up his gut would get stuck behind the big steering wheel, and she'd just shrug and take her seat, and Darly and Joey would laugh and say, "Fuckin'-A right, Suzy, go tell that fat fuck where to plug it."

She didn't exactly know when anything like that would happen, so until then she simply blended in with the other strangers on the 502 Lidice route, with the older people coming and going to work, and the very old people who scowled and shook their heads and whispered whenever the kids got wild with the laughing and swearing that made Suzy sort of proud that she was young like they were. Then she would wonder about what Busha would say if she were riding the bus home with her, hearing how the older kids yelled and cursed, how Joey Korosa and Darly Shapinka would tongue-kiss and feel each other up right there in front of everybody, and how *she* wanted to be the one tongue-kissing Joey, and how it would make Busha so sick and upset and afraid for her granddaughter that Suzy didn't even want to think about it.

16

The bus stop was down the hill by the plant at the corner market called Garnsey's, where everyone went to pay the telephone, gas, and electric bills. The sun was strong, probably the warmest so far that season, and the hot exhaust actually smelled sweet as the bus rumbled away and the students shoved one another off the curb and along the sidewalk. Some days Suzy walked ahead of this group, some days absently among them, and some days, like this day, she kept her pace slowly behind them, turning once or twice to watch Joey and Darly walk off in the opposite direction. They trudged away in crooked steps, hunched forward with their hands in their pockets like two sick hoboes desperately trying to get out of the afternoon.

Suzy knew that if she, and not Darly Shapinka, were to walk home with Joey, his step would straighten and his face would open up smiling in the sunlight. She was sure of it, so sure that she walked backwards for many steps to get one last look at them, at him, before they turned a corner and disappeared until she saw them in each other's arms on the bus the next morning.

But it was just then, as the crowd of students walked past the main gate in front of Joliet Washer and Wire, that Suzy decided with complete certainty to introduce herself to Joey Korosa by going to the Zimne Piwo Club by herself on Good Friday. She was immediately satisfied with the bravery of her decision, yet her happiness only lasted for a few seconds when it was split by a commotion of yelling somewhere in the plant that she instantly recognized as disaster. Everyone stopped.

Someone from the plant yelled, "Move it! Move it!"

"You kids move back, back!" another man yelled. "Make room!"

The exit signal buzzed and the crowd backed away from the gate when it opened, and through it walked a cluster of men carrying someone. Their plant clothes were splattered with blood.

Because Suzy had already prepared herself to see something awful, she first took in bits of this image through a few long moments before she slowly built them into a complete and terrible panorama—the crowd of students on the sunny street, the opening gate, the blood-splattered clothes, the men who wore them, and, finally, who the men were carrying, who was bloodier than any of them, stained from his feet to his face with streaks of his own bright blood, who was sobbing, who was rolling his head around and moaning Shit and *Jesus* over and over.

When the kids saw Mickey Grogan being carried out like this, they backed even further into the street and one of them said, "God-fucking-damn!" The men lowered Mickey down on the sidewalk, and one of them touched his head and whispered soothingly, pouting into his ear like a mother.

One of the students asked, "Hey, what happened to him?" and one of the men answered, "Caught his hand in a machine." Another kid asked, "What kind of machine? Hey, what kind of machine?" but none of the men seemed to hear the question.

Suzy's first impulse at the sight of all the blood and the sound of Mickey Grogan's wailing wasn't disgust, nor was it pity. It was simple, angry shame. She was sure that he'd been drinking on the job, just as he'd been drunk the last time she saw him waving to her from the Zimne Piwo Club, and hammered to hell the night he walked with her and rambled through his rotten breath, then tongued her mouth as he grabbed at her. Now she could see that the very same hand was wrapped in a ball of towels pulsing with blood, so much blood that soon the ball no longer looked like cloth at all, but like a fresh organ still twitching from the life it had been cut from.

Mickey Grogan writhed on the sidewalk and clutched his forearm, skinny and very white against the lines of blood that ran down it. He raised his head then and yelled, "Aw, Jesus H. Christ this hurts so bad, this hurts so goddamn bad I'm gonna die!"

More men came from the gate to look at Mickey and shake their heads and wonder where the hell the goddamn ambulance was. When it finally came, Suzy watched the paramedics strap Mickey, a pale green now, eyes closed, onto the stretcher and slide him into the back with a quick slam before they sped away to Silver Cross Hospital.

Plant accidents were not unusual at Joliet Washer and Wire, and so it didn't take long for the shock of that scene to pass for any of them. It was, after all, something to talk about for everyone else who hadn't gotten his hand torn to hell in one of the bolt strippers. The students headed home gabbing enthusiastically about the blood and the sobbing, and the plant workers shuffled back to their shifts after some cigarettes and talk about the harness trifectas that ran the night before at Balmoral.

This had not been the worst thing Suzy had ever seen either, and as she walked up the hill toward Pulaski Street behind the rest of the them, she thought about how cancer had shriveled her Dzia Dzia down to sixty pounds, and how she had watched him near the end in his bed defecate out of his mouth, nearly choking, while Busha wiped the shit from his lips with a rag, just as she did when thin green liquid would dribble in a steady stream from his nose. The same Dzia Dzia who had danced with Busha in their tiny kitchen to the polka station on the little AM radio by the stove on Saturday afternoons whenever Suzy went to see them.

As for Mickey Grogan, Suzy felt an underdeveloped sense of vindication for having had to endure one awful night of his breath, lips, hands, and blubbering. Of all the older boys around, why hadn't Joey Korosa been the one to cross the street that night to walk with her? She wouldn't have even cared if he'd been drunk.

She would have liked him drunk. She would have pulled herself into his arms as they slowly strolled down the darkened sidewalks, and he wouldn't have smelled like Mickey Grogan, and she would have kissed him as much as he wanted. But he hadn't been Joey. He had been sick Mickey Grogan, and soon she just stopped thinking about him and let the sun liven her warm daydreams about Good Friday and the chances it would bring her to get even closer to Joey.

Fat Kuputzniak was sweeping the sidewalk in front of his tavern as Suzy walked past. He did not look up at her or any of the other students until one of them said, "Hey, Fat, you hear about Mickey Grogan?"

"Yeah, I heard," he said, focusing again on the broken glass and dust he swept off the walk with slow annoyance. "What a yard of cuntluck. That kid spends a lot of money in my place."

School let out for Easter vacation on Holy Thursday. On the way home, the 502 Lidice route driver had to pull the bus over and tell all the kids on board to quiet the hell down and quit the horsing around or else he'd kick every goddamn one of them off and make them walk home in the rain.

Suzy grabbed the seat in front of her, raised herself to glare at the driver. What the hell did he expect? Easter Vacation was on and everyone was excited. He couldn't kick everyone off. They'd all paid to ride. "But we already paid the goddamn fare," she called out, her voice measured and sharp though the tremble in her chest fought to batter the words down to a flattened retreat. She hadn't planned on impressing Darly and Joey this day, and yelling at the driver just happened to come up as the chance to do so before Good Friday, which was tomorrow. She waited to see what would happen next. At the high school the teachers would write you up for this kind of backtalk. The official charge was Disrespect and Defiance of Authority. She already felt different, felt tough and proud, brave to be the only one to stand up for the rest of them.

A little yellow woman in a black raincoat two seats down glared at her. The driver squinted a hard look in his wide rearview mirror. Nobody said a thing for a brief but worthwhile moment; the rumbling idle of the motionless bus engine and the steady patter of rain on the windows magnified the weight of that silence.

The driver finally made a sound in his nose that was supposed to be a laugh and said, "I don't care if you own the goddamn bus. When I'm driving you gotta keep it down back there. It's the law." He pulled away from the curb and, shaking his head, thrust the bus back into traffic.

Suzy of course hadn't been the source of any racket, hadn't actually said a word since she'd gotten on board that afternoon, nor for that matter in all the months she'd ridden the 502 Lidice route to and from the high school each day, and so when she had spoken up—the new crass advocate for a group that had nearly nothing to do with her outside of age and destination, now Suzy was even embarrassed that the gesture might be taken by the older kids, most importantly by Darly Shapinka and Joey Korosa, as an immature, needy, ambitiously obvious way to attract their attention, but keenly waiting just the same for some sign that at least one of them appreciated her brave response, as in a real laugh or a knuckle to her shoulder—the silent stares that sliced through her from every narrow direction on the bus seemed set not exactly in surprise, but in the astonished realization that she was even there in the first place.

Joey and Darly hadn't even heard a thing. They'd been arguing a few minutes before, and now Darly was weeping by herself, waiting for Joey to gather her up with apology. His back to her several seats away, he slumped down with his arms crossed and eyed the rain drenched windows and let the turns and bumps of the bus rock him into a half-sleep.

And when nobody spoke to or even looked at Suzy for the rest of the ride, or afterwards on the shivering walk from Garnsey's up to Pulaski Street, first past the plant that seemed completely vacant under the gray rush of the rain, the downpour now gushing down the hill in a chilly wash that filled her shoes and drenched her feet numb, Suzy Kosasovich felt a strange new squeeze of humiliation that instructed her to understand her place among the older kids on the bus. Her place among Joey and Darly. Which was no place. She was a sort of Busha already and she belonged alongside the other old friendless and forgotten women who dressed in black and filled the aisles of Saint Cyril's for any opportunity to pray for a tranquil end in death to the misery of neglect. She deeply regretted opening her mouth, and wondered why suddenly she cared so much about what the older kids thought of her. She finally had to admit that she had always cared, had pined for their attention, and had kept herself from them each day simply because as long as she said nothing there would always be a chance to say something that was perfect and original, that would captivate and thrill everyone into adoring her very presence there among them.

When Suzy got home, Busha leaped from her living room seat where she sat alone each day fingering her rosary and waiting for the moving, speaking life of her family to pour back into the house. She smothered Suzy with kisses, "My Good Angel, My Good Angel," and asked her about her day, her studies, her appetite, then turned Suzy around to pull off her coat and gabbled about how wet Suzy was, how cold, and how she was going to die of pneumonia if she didn't get upstairs right now and change into something dry and warm.

"Oh, my God, please!" Suzy said, pulling herself away, the first time she had ever spoken to Busha like that, and the first time Busha's care had actually provoked rage. She immediately felt horrible, and covered her mouth and looked at her grandmother, who seemed more confused than hurt.

"Okay, okay," Busha said, turning for her seat. "Just go change upstairs please. For your Busha who loves you."

The next morning, Suzy still felt bad about the way she had snapped at Busha, so as soon as she got up she helped her cover the holy statues and icons throughout the house in accordance with Good Friday's solemn observance, then took her to Saint Cyril's for Veneration of the Cross, where all the saints and their altars were covered with purple shrouds, and the weeping old lined up to kiss the feet of Christ on the enormous wooden crucifix Father Zajc and two altar boys held at the end of the aisle, the boys wiping Christ's spiked, bloody feet with silk after each wrinkled congregant bent to press her trembling lips against the greenish plaster.

When it was Suzy's turn, she had the terrifying urge to spit all over Jesus's feet, just to make everyone hate her even more. She had long decided against going to the Zimne Piwo Club that day, but as she and Busha passed it on the way home later that afternoon, the rain gone and the sun strong again and even hotter against the pavement, Suzy was seized with the realization that Pulaski Street had been momentarily taken over by the very young and the very old. Small, slow groups of old women were all walking home from church, righteous and proud of their stomach pangs from Good Friday fasting, some still weeping, wishing out loud that they might suffer a pain in death as great as the Savior's, while bigger, louder groups of the young (she saw Joey and Darly leaning stiff-mouthed against somebody's Pontiac) were prowling around in their jeans and T-shirts and short skirts, smoking in the sun and lining up in front of the tavern, already yelling and drunk rough though they hadn't yet had a drop, and there in front of the bar Suzy moved with Busha, head down, between these two alliances that either feared or ignored one another (the latter smirking, spitting quick curses that burned the air and made the old women sick, that anyone should say such things on the day of the Lord's Blessed Agony; she heard Darly Shapinka somewhere behind her say, *He can go fuck himself*), and decided that if she didn't go to the Zimne Piwo Club that day after all, she would always be part of the small, slow group that padded along the outskirts of a good time, that stayed inside on Friday nights watching television and shivering as the windows shook from the gusts of fast, packed cars blasting music and liquor laughter, a thought that angered Suzy into picking up her pace to get Busha home as quickly as she could.

"Hold on, hold on," Busha said. "Why you going so fast, My Good Angel?"

Once she had Busha back in her living room seat counting her rosary beads, Suzy ran upstairs and painted herself and pulled back her hair into a tight shiny ponytail, ditched her church clothes, then dashed back down to face Busha when she got up and asked, "Where you going?"

"I've gotta go for a walk."

"Today? But it's Good Friday. You wearing your relic I gave you?"

"Yes," Suzy said, then bent her head and found the relic down her shirt and gently took it out to show Busha, who squinted and looked closely at Saint Rufina's swatch of tattered garment as if to make sure it had not yet started its own miraculous bleeding.

Then Busha said, "Where you going to walk to?"

"I don't know," Suzy said. "I'll be back later. Bye, Busha," she said, leaving the old woman standing in the middle of the empty living room, her lips downturned and parted in simple worry, her stare obscured behind the glaze of light that reflected off her glasses, the crucifix on the end of her rosary beads dangling by her small, slippered feet.

Smoke from the plant hung behind the green shingled rooftops and budding trees along Pulaski Street. A barge horn moaned up the hill from the canal, and bells sounded from the guard gate on the Ruby Street bridge. Suzy slowly made her way toward the Zimne Piwo Club, stepping over streams of soapy water that ran from a few short concrete driveways where retired men in white undershirts washed their Pontiacs and Buicks with sponges and buckets of garden hose water, then let them dry in the sun while they sat on their porches drinking beer, listening to the daily race results from Arlington on tinny transistors before they rose again to slowly wax their cars under the warm and easy beam of beer. Their cars always looked far better kept than the scabby yards and rusted fences that surrounded their dumb little houses where they wasted the last years of their defeated lives by talking to each other about how well their cars were running, though they had absolutely no place to go. Aside from Busha and dead Dzia Dzia, Suzy decided that she hated all the world's old completely, and these old car washing men in particular. She noticed them watching her as she passed, and she knew what they thought about when they looked at her: a choice slice of tail they might have gotten had time not sucked away any chance for just one crack. At least she wasn't ugly; she knew her form had already developed in the way that always made men stare, especially old bored men. This cheap awareness of her own body gave her an edge of confidence she needed badly that afternoon, a confidence that slipped further and further from her imagination the closer she got to the Zimne Piwo Club, and to all the groups of the normally forbidden young moving freely in and out of it. Some of them sat on boxes of beer and chugged from paper bags of canned Old Style under wisps of cigarette smoke, and some took turns shoving each other into the steady sprinkle of water that dribbled down from the air cooling unit on the second story apartment window where Fat Kuputzniak lived when he wasn't tending bar, the rusty drops battering the concrete into a dented circle of permanent brown rings.

She saw, but did not watch, Joey Korosa and Darly Shapinka leaning together against the Pontiac. The car was parked across Pulaski Street, and a few guys she didn't know were watching with Darly and Joey the foolish excitement and drama of young people suddenly given to something they wanted, but didn't really know how to take. Suzy felt much more securely advanced than that. So securely advanced that she forced herself not to react when she saw, but did not watch, Darly Shapinka kiss Joey full on the lips, saw Joey hold Darly in the warmth of the sunlight.

Few seemed to notice Suzy approach. Only two nasty younger girls and an ugly boy she didn't know quieted and mumbled something about her that she refused to hear, just as she refused to look at them lest her glance betray the very terror that compelled her to count each cautious step, until she was finally facing the small window on the front door, the only window to that place. The glass was covered over with an old coat of black paint that was chipped and peeling so that dim dots and slices of light passed through like fading stars in a small, polluted universe.

The room she entered was for many seconds an even darker universe that gradually took shape as her eyes adjusted from sunlight to barlight: tables and booths cluttered in a narrow length of space that led back to a slightly wider room with a pool table, shuffleboard, dart board, and then again to the main part of the bar where shapes of faces were forming now at the tables, in the booths, some along the long bar, every face too young to be there drinking beer (they were all drinking beer; the harder shots of killmixed liquor came later that night when the crowd pressed itself in over every inch of space and body heat stank from the sweating walls of that place), the faces eventually acquiring their features, mouths that whispered about her and stared (there was nothing to hear anyway but the jukebox music, something country crackling from it now just for laughs, the rare redneck tune among disc after disk of hokey polkas that the kids hated only a little less), and eyes that lowered and then parted as they watched her standing there in the doorway.

One of those faces was rounded, pocked, topped with a thinning gray shine of oil-dressed hair above eyes ringed with pockets of fat the color of cigarette ash, and belonged to the lone proprietor of this dump where nothing—glasses, bottles, tables, walls, girly beer posters, booth vinyl, billiard felt, cue sticks—nothing was the color it was supposed to be, but bleached and yellowed and chipped and faded, regal only through the jeweled lenses of coruscated ethanolic delusion, sitting at the far end of the bar by himself next to a half-empty bottle of brandless white liquor in a silver bowl of ice, his weight slumped on meaty arms crossed on the long wooden bar that was stained with dull white circles where thousands of sweaty glasses had sat, had been lifted and guzzled from, and had been set back down empty for only a second before they were filled fresh again to repeat this soggy cycle a thousand more times.

Suzy made her way to the bar and positioned herself on a stool. Fat Kuputzniak stood, burped into his fist, winced, lumbered toward her without smiling, then burped into his fist again and said, "Pick your poison, Flower."

For some time, Suzy felt so displayed and self-conscious there at the bar that she could only stare down at her flattish yellow beer and count the beads of moisture that occasionally ran down the glass. All but two stools along the bar were taken, and those two were on either side of Suzy. She was relieved, since she wouldn't know what to say to either person who might sit in them. When she finally did look up, she was surprised to see how loud and packed the tavern had actually gotten. She recognized so many kids from the bus that she flinched and braced herself for the lurch that would come when the bar pulled away from the curb.

When she spotted Darly Shapinka sitting on Joey Korosa's lap at a cramped table through the crowd, she snapped back around and slurped down the rest of her beer.

The second one was much easier to drink. She was still the only one there by herself, but she no longer felt so prominently alone. The empty stools had been taken and turned away, dozens were crowding up to the bar to get beers, and Fat Kuputzniak was filling their glasses as slowly and angrily as he could, sometimes stopping whatever he was doing to stumble back to his silver bowl of liquor where he would sit and drink for as long as he fuckin' felt like it, making everyone packed up at the bar wait until he was good and goddamn ready, knowing none of them could complain or take their business elsewhere. And so as Suzy sipped her second beer, she was calm enough to watch this scene through her first beer buzz ever, a thrilling bloom of warmer blood that started in her head and rushed straight to her gut like a gift.

The door opened and closed many times and tossed in flashes of the pink sun setting duller and duller until the only light that came in was from the blue band on the Old Style sign out front. Zimne Piwo Club, the sign said. Old Style On Tap—Na Zarowie!

She glanced at the sign each time the door opened, read the words to herself, never daring to turn and look at Joey with Darly Shapinka each time she heard her rough laugh, and soon she didn't care about who Joey had on his lap, didn't care about who he or anyone else liked to screw. She was sitting in a bar completely by herself. What other girl her age had that kind of spine? And it was Friday night, finally Friday night, and she was feeling her first good light buzz, and *Aw, fuck all you Joliet losers!* she felt like yelling, and there was a pack of cigarettes next to her that belonged to some girl who wasn't looking, and she took one and lit it and smoked and slugged back her second beer, and was just about to wave Fat Kuputzniak over for a third when somebody big squeezed himself up to the bar right next to her and said, "Christ, that Kuputzniak moves in two speeds. Slow and goddamn stop."

When Suzy looked up and saw Joey Korosa, a wave of fright crashed inside and almost brought all the beer back up. She wasn't sure if he had actually spoken to her until he asked her if she had another cigarette, and she was so stunned and honored by the ease of his question that she laughed without even trying and said, "Oh, yeah, no, I stole it."

"Forget it," he said, producing his own pack of red Marlboros. "I just wanted to see what I could get off you for free."

This hurt her, but when she answered, "You're just a jerk, then," she instantly regretted how childishly silly and unconvincing it sounded, and thought that Joey might just shrug and leave her right where he found her.

But he didn't leave. Nor did he laugh, apologize, or give any hint that he'd even heard her. He smoked, watched Fat Kuputzniak, waited for him to notice his empty glass. Suzy feared that he'd already forgotten her, so she loudly and eagerly announced, "Hey, I seen you on the bus. You go to Joliet West, don't you."

"Yep," he said, without looking down at her. She couldn't think of any other voice in the world, not from television or from any movie she'd ever seen, that sounded like Joey Korosa's voice, a deep cream of voice that she greedily wanted to hear more of, and a feverish worry flared in her face as she fidgeted and scrambled for something else to say.

"So how old are you?" he asked, and Suzy was so thrilled by the question that at once she wanted to tell him everything she'd ever imagined about him, how different and smart and *artistic* he would be once he finished school and moved up to the *sophistication* of a big busy place like Chicago, and how she would love him in ways that none of these losers ever would.

"Fourteen," Suzy answered.

Joey shook his head and, without looking at her, letting one side of his mouth curl into a reluctant smile, said, "I'm a lot older than you."

"So what?" she said, and laughed. "Who cares? It's Good Friday. Jesus died for you."

This made Joey laugh a little, and then Fat Kuputzniak came over and nodded for Joey's order.

"Want another beer?" Joey asked her.

"Sure, and a shot of vodka," she said, having absolutely no idea what vodka tasted like, nor how hard it would hit her, yet knowing she would have gladly slurped down a jar of gasoline to impress Joey into recognizing how daring she actually was.

He handed the drinks to her and raised his glass for a toast. "So what's your name?" Joey Korosa asked her.

"Suzy Kosasovich," she said.

"To Suzy Kosasovich," he said.

The shot of vodka burned, but Suzy was too excited to let it bother her, especially when Joey asked her if she wanted to come sit with him and his friends, an offer she pretended to consider for about ten glorious seconds before she said, "Why not? Sure, yeah."

She hopped down from her stool and followed Joey through the tight crowd that chattered and laughed with each other under the nerdy verve of jukebox polka, better than no music at all given the hassle-free beer and bar space for one night, the crowd parting for big crazy Joey Korosa and glancing with interest at the young girl who must have been bad enough to get an invite to sit with him at all.

Suzy couldn't help smiling within this spinning nimbus of booze and sudden attention, and she didn't care about how she must have looked, blushing behind such a crazy smile, because she couldn't remember when she had felt so hopeful and expectant, when such a smile was so impossible to contain. She was close enough to Joey to see the muscles in his back move underneath his black T-shirt, and the few slick curls of dark hair against his smooth, strong neck.

They were almost to his table, and when Joey stepped aside, Suzy saw the few others who were there waiting for him: some grimy guys she didn't know with long hair and patched leather jackets, and, sitting there with her arms crossed, her eyes heavily painted, her meaty scowl glistening with a thick coat of pink lipstick, glaring right through Suzy with straight hatred, was Darly Shapinka.

"Who the fuck is she?" Darly asked, and Suzy looked away to the door just as it opened for the comfort of the blue light of the familiar words, Old Style On Tap—Na Zarowie! But comfort was the last thing she felt when, illuminated by that same blue light, in walked Mickey Grogan, alone, crouching into the doorway, nervously eyeing the tavern, a football-sized wad of white bandages wrapped tightly around his injured hand.

Within seconds he spotted Suzy, bloomed with a big stupid smile, waved his bandaged hand over his head and called out to her. "Suzy! Hey, Suzy!"

Joey Korosa had already gotten an extra chair for her, and was standing by his table talking to Darly, who was still staring furiously at Suzy, then yelling at Joey, scowling and shaking her head.

"How the hell are you, Suzy?" Mickey Grogan asked, a lamely musical uncle-chum cheer in his greeting. His face actually looked fuller than she remembered, but his breath was still plain awful, a hot fecal breeze through his rotten teeth. "Listen, listen," he said, "I've wanted to talk to you so bad about what I did that one night, and I want you to know that I'm sorry. I was pretty drunk and—"

"Forget it," Suzy snapped. Her empty chair was waiting at Joey's table. But so was Darly Shapinka, arms crossed, leering, furious, painted, evil, ready as ever to kick some bitch's ass. Ready as ever to kick Suzy's ass all over the bar while Suzy hopelessly crawled across the floor, bawling, while the crowd made room and cheered.

"So how's your hand?" she asked Mickey, to distract herself.

His response lasted several minutes. But Suzy only caught the last part. She felt dizzy and hot with alcohol, with want, threat, and annoyance, while Mickey Grogan jabbered about how well his hand was doing, gesturing, shrugging, pointing to different parts of the bandage wrapped around it, a mouthless hand puppet without eyes performing a retarded dance in the middle of the Zimne Piwo Club, in the middle of the swaying, pushing crowd that moved with sweaty, inadvertent waves to the bellowing jukebox polkas, her empty chair right next to Joey, who kept smiling and waving her over, while Darly kept staring, then angrily barking into Joey's ear, and somehow Suzy had another cigarette going, had finished her beer and somehow already had another one in her hand, and then, right as she decided that any risk was a risk worth taking if it meant getting closer to Joey, she caught the very end of Mickey Grogan's rank, spit-drenched speech: "My fingers are growing back right now, right inside the bandage! No kidding, Suzy. They stuck my fingers to one of my legs in the hospital and the skin's gonna make my fingers like new. Like goddamn new!"

"I've gotta go sit with my friends," Suzy told him. "See you around."

Mickey asked her if he could sit with them too, but Suzy was already on her way, already thrusting herself for Joey Korosa's table when she felt Mickey trying to follow her, the fool, deciding she'd rather risk a beating from Darly Shapinka than listen to another minute of his grating, friendly friend-talk. Then she imagined Joey proudly rescuing her from Darly, lovingly taking her out of that noisy bar and down to the spot under the black train bridge this side of the barge canal where they could finally be totally alone in the dark.

"What the hell took you so long?" Joey asked, slapping the empty seat twice before he slugged back the rest of his beer and dropped his cigarette butt into the bottle. Darly didn't acknowledge Suzy, but held the same forcefully absent look in her face that she wore whenever she was about to cry by herself on the bus after fighting with Joey: conspicuously alone, gazing at nothing, indignantly silent, the only way Darly knew how to attract attention outside of flaunting her big tits, swearing, and making ugly threats. Suzy was glad she wasn't her.

Joey introduced the others at the table. This was Coonan, this was Ape Drape. They lived down in Rockdale and worked at Kuluzni Brothers, canning lard, and they'd been Joey's boys for years. Suzy pretended she was glad to meet them.

And this was Darly Shapinka.

"Hi," Suzy said.

Darly nodded once, but she wouldn't look at Suzy, and Suzy knew that Darly was intimidated by her arrival, which made her feel a little relieved and superior. Darly suddenly became much sadder in Suzy's eye. Pathetic. All talk. She wanted another shot of vodka, another beer, another cigarette, until Darly finally faced her and said, "Yeah, I seen you on the bus but I always thought you were retarded or something."

Someone standing behind Suzy said, "No, no, she ain't retarded," and when she looked up and saw that Mickey Grogan had been hovering there the whole time, she stood to leave. But then Joey grabbed her arm and said, "Hey, come on, Darly's just drunk," and the warmth of his grip and the want in his voice settled her back to her seat and made Darly disappear for a moment.

"And who the fuck asked you, spazz?" Joey said to Mickey. "Go pick the goddamn scabs off your hand."

Coonan and Ape Drape laughed. One of them said, "Yeah, go eat your fucking scabs, man."

"Let us know if they taste any better than boogers, jagoff," said the other, and Suzy laughed louder than any of them as Mickey left their table with no response beyond staring deadpan at the crowd he walked through to go stand by himself at the jukebox.

Joey leaned over to say something to Darly, and she rolled her eyes and told him to go fuck himself, he wasn't her goddamn father, then grabbed her beer and stumbled away.

"She's just drunk," Joey said, his eyes a little puffy and his grin mean. "Shit, but so am I," he said, and laughed in a way that wasn't meant to be shared with anyone but himself. Suzy caught herself staring at him, and when she glanced away through a part in the crowd she saw Darly at the bar, craning her neck to stare right back. Then Darly was talking to two older-looking guys Suzy didn't recognize. They looked like they were in college, or jock preps from Joliet Catholic High. Izod shirts tucked into white jeans, rich jock assholes. They didn't belong there, and everyone else was eying them too. Suzy didn't care; they were keeping Darly occupied, and now she was taking her place right next to Joey. The preps bought Darly a drink and stared at her tits as she hoisted them onto the bar, leaning against it.

Suzy wondered if Joey would react, but all he did was ease his arm around her and say, "So, Suzy, how come I never saw you on the bus?"

"I hide under the seats," she said, and Joey smiled and put his hand on her leg, and Darly wasn't watching any more and Joey's friends had left them to get drinks. She had everything she needed just sitting here right next to Joey, and she actually tried to tell him this, braced herself and said it, but Joey was lighting another cigarette and he didn't hear her under the brass blast *wha wha wha* that roared from the jukebox. Louder, she said, "Hey, do you want to go somewhere?"

"What?"

"Do you want to go somewhere else?"

"Why?"

Suzy shrugged, disappointed that he hadn't caught on. "Somewhere where we can talk." Then she got brave and said, "Somewhere where we can be alone."

"Sure, but not right yet," he said. "My boys are still here and all. I'm having a pretty good time."

Joey's friends came back with beers and bourbon shots for everyone, and because Joey had said "Sure," Suzy even relished how terribly the booze burned her throat when she knocked back her shot with the others. She choked back the urge to cough and spit in light of joyously knowing that she and Joey would finally be alone sometime later that night. "Sure," he had said.

"How's it taste?" Joey asked her.

"Sure," she said, and Joey and his friends all laughed, and they all drank down their chasers and laughed some more and lit cigarettes, and for a second Suzy caught Mickey Grogan watching her from the jukebox, just watching with no kind of face but a watching one, but she ignored this since Joey had his hand on her leg, squeezing higher and higher up her thigh, and she asked him again to come on, let's go somewhere and be alone, and again he said, "Sure, but not right yet. Later."

"You're an artist!" she announced, and this time none of the guys at the table laughed; they snickered and looked at each other and shook their heads.

"Artist, yes, well," one of Joey's friends said with deepened mock maturity, Ape Train or Eight Train, whatever his goddamn name was, and Suzy wanted to tell him and his other little snickering scumbag buddy to fuck off and leave her with her man. Alone. And the only reason Joey was snickering too was because his friends were there.

"You *are* an artist, Joey," Suzy insisted. "An artist for real. A painter." She figured this was how older people talked when they sat around drinking, so who cared about Joey's friends?

"I am an artist," Joey said with a slur. "I'm a fuck artist. I got my own fuck museum down the block."

None of them could stop laughing, and Suzy knew she had become the center of their joke, the bastards, and Joey was just a bastard too, and then the bourbon rushed to her head and tears came to her eyes and she kept herself from sobbing by focusing on the red ashtray in the middle of Joey's table, a red circle with four little cigarette dents surrounding a dirty, smoldering heap of crushed and twisted filters.

"Oh shit," one of them said. "She's gonna puke," and Suzy was glad they didn't know how hurt she was. Joey quickly got up to get her some water while his friends rubbed her back and said, "Breathe through your nose. There you go. Close one. Fuckin'-A."

Suzy had been no where near throwing up, so when she asked for another shot, and drank it, Joey and his friends laughed and praised her quick recovery.

On any other Friday night the Zimne Piwo Club would have been occupied by their uncles and fathers. After work. Before work. Between shifts. They'd play a dice game called barbudi, watch the White Sox, drink, and tell jokes about niggers and pussy. They'd get soaked, sure, flat out fucking soused, and sometimes guys got hot and shoved each other, but Christ, they all worked together, had grown up together, so fights got stopped before they even started, and whatever happened happened and was soon resolved and forgotten.

That Friday night, Good Friday night, none of them came to the Zimne Piwo Club. Many of them were taking extra shifts at the plant, but those who weren't simply went to other taverns in Crest Hill, Rockdale, and Preston Heights. They knew what happened to Fat Kuputzniak every year, and they all thought it was a sick drag the way he got so stewed and let all those kids in to drink, no matter how down he got from remembering his little dead sister. It wasn't right. But deeper in their judgment was knowing that their own sons, daughters, nieces, and nephews were all packed inside the Zimne Piwo Club getting stewed right with Fat Kuputzniak, and what the hell could any of them do about it anyway? So all the uncles and fathers who weren't taking extra shifts told their wives they were, loaded up into somebody's car, and drank elsewhere. Hell, there might be some pussy at the next bar, some drunk and sloppy strange at the next joint, and they'd have a good goddamn time no matter what, and there might be a party after the bars closed, more drinking until dawn with a little cocaine, a gangbang with the sloppy strange, so when Good Friday finally rolled around and they knew they wouldn't be drinking at the Zimne Piwo Club on account of Fat Kuputzniak and all those goddamn kids, disappointment was actually the last thing any of them felt.

One of the two jock preps at the bar said something wrong to Darly Shapinka and she smashed a bottle against his head. He collapsed and blood poured over his face. His buddy slapped at Darly with a limp and untried fist, missed, and swung again. Then Darly stepped back and the prep tried to kick at her, but he just lost his ground and fell flat on his ass. The laughter that followed was so thunderous no one heard the strangers screaming for Christ when Coonan, Ape Drape, and a bunch of other guys dragged, beat, and kicked them into the street and didn't come back for a long time.

Suzy didn't know how long they were gone, and she wasn't keeping track of the minutes. She was letting Joey's hand reach around her, then up her shirt and under her bra to toy with her nipples. She couldn't believe it. She wanted to laugh. Both her breasts were all the way out under her shirt, right in the middle of the bar. Under the table, Joey kept pressing her hand against his thing, all stiff inside his jeans. She loved him even more because he hadn't gotten up to save Darly when the prep tried to hit her. She too had laughed when the poor guy fell down under his own kick, even though she had wanted him to smash Darly Shapinka right there in front of everybody. Nobody would have missed that pig anyway.

The jukebox was getting louder, the polka music blowing from it older and older and more disgusting. She thought about getting up and unplugging the goddamn thing, then Joey pinched her nipple too hard and she squealed. She laughed and remembered she had a whole beer in front of her. She took it in both hands and drank it, and when she put the glass back down Joey grabbed her hand and stuck it under the table and onto his leg, into his fly, over his thing, and she wasn't sure about what she was really supposed to do with it, so she just squeezed and squeezed, and eventually Joey took his hand away from hers and seemed to be settled on liking the way she squeezed it. He breathed hard and made a noise, a small groan. Right there in the middle of the bar. And when the jukebox got even louder, more embarrassing, she looked over at it and saw Mickey Grogan and his big stupid bandage leaning into the machine, studying the song titles, pressing the buttons, dropping in quarters, mumbling to himself in the dull, colored strobes of festive jukebox light with a fixed and deliberate sneer, the same look he kept locked in place as he slowly turned his head to leer at her.

Darly had found her way back to the table. "Go get me a drink, Joey," she said. "Go get me a drink, pussylover. Cocksucker," she said.

"Go get it yourself," Joey told her.

Then Darly clutched the back of Suzy's seat, swung down to her ear and, with much slurring, said, "Look, I don't know who you think you are coming in here and flashing your little bald pussy around, but Joey's my goddamn man. I could have beat your ass in by now, but I'm warning you instead, you know?"

Joey grabbed Darly's arm and dragged her away through the crowd toward the bar. She tripped over herself and her rear rippled from the jolt in great waves of dumpy fat.

Mickey Grogan hurried to the table when he saw that Suzy was finally sitting alone. "Hey," he said. "What she say to you, Suzy? I saw her say something."

"God," Suzy said, waving her hand in front of her nose. "Get away. Go brush your teeth. Do you eat out of the toilet or something?"

Mickey pulled a chair out, sat, then touched her arm and said, "Listen, you know I'm your friend."

"No you're not," Suzy told him, shrugging his hand away.

"No, listen," Mickey said. "Maybe you drank too much. I seen you drinking a lot tonight, and I didn't even think you ever drank anything. I had to stop drinking. I haven't had nothing to drink at all since my accident, you know. Now listen."

Suzy didn't listen, but worried with a sudden and anxious awareness of herself. Maybe she *was* too drunk, and maybe drinking was making her too mean. She had, with utterly selfish cruelty, laughed at Mickey when Joey and his friends told him to pick and eat his scabs. His scabs. She had never in her life laughed so carelessly at anyone else's suffering, and all in one night, this night, she had made up for her lifetime of quiet reservation and kindness. No, it hadn't been just this night, but lately. She knew she could be just as mean without liquor, like when she had yelled at Busha the afternoon before. And what had Busha ever done to anyone but work herself into exhaustion from limitless love and care? She imagined Busha where she had left her that day: standing alone in the empty house with nothing to do but pray on her beads. She was probably praying for Suzy this instant, and here Suzy sat with her breasts hanging out under her shirt, and very drunk, and longing for someone who freely fucked whomever he wanted, who sniffed cocaine, drank, took pills. Jesus, how Busha would sob in her slow sad-old-lady way if she knew where Suzy was, if she knew what her Good Angel really wanted. She felt for the relic in her shirt when she forgot that it had been there all along. It had gotten caught in the folds of her bra when Joey pulled the cups down over her nipples, then completely off. Now the bra was stretched and twisted around her middle, and the underwires were taut and squeezed against the tender skin under her breasts. Suzy understood that she had the power to hurt people needlessly, and, light in the brain with her first booze ever, this severely depressed and shamed her.

"So no matter what happens," Mickey continued. "You know you've got a friend here is what I'm saying."

One whiff of Mickey's green reek breath slapped her out of dwelling on the gloom of drunken guilt. She was annoyed and disgusted by him all over again. His accident, his bandage, his leering and waiting in the jukebox wings for a moment to sneak his way over just to tongue and grab her, his idiot boner twitching away in his jeans.

She saw Joey over at the bar. Coonan and Ape Drape had come back, and Joey was talking to them. There was no sign of Darly anywhere. Maybe, Suzy thought, Darly had finally gone home, and now she had Joey Korosa all to herself, and maybe soon they'd leave to be alone, and to hell with how mean she'd been. Everybody has a bad day. Everybody barks sometimes. She wasn't that awful—wasn't Darly Shapinka, and she sure as hell wasn't Mickey Grogan.

She stood up and said, "I didn't come here to listen to your bullshit all night."

Mickey's mouth dropped into a parted quiver of hurt. "Oh, Suzy, wait," he said. "I just wanted you to know how sorry I was. I didn't mean anything."

"They should lock you up," Suzy said. "You'd have raped me that night if I couldn't walk so fast."

"No, no, Suzy. No way, no way," he said.

He tried to follow her through the crowd, yelling, "Wait, Suzy. Please," but when he saw where she was headed, he stopped flat and pushed his way back over to the jukebox, where he scratched his head and squinted at the spinning discs and cursed himself for every mistake he'd ever made.

Joey blew a thin puff of cigarette smoke and, through it, watched Suzy come to him. He winked and grinned and asked her if she wanted another smoke, a beer, a shot. She gladly took all three, a senseless belt that drenched her brain and made the rest of the room darken with a garbled blur. She fell back onto the bar—slack-eyed, sour, and salivating with nausea. Puking would just ruin everything. Joey would never kiss her with puke all over her breath. The minutes were closing in on her chances. "Joey, let's go," she said. "Please. Let's just go now."

For the rest of the night, Suzy moved in and out of this condition, depending on the sequence and severity of events that passed before her. She plodded from stool to booth, from table to wall, sometimes with Joey, only Joey, and sometimes with Joey and his stupid Rockdale friends, and sometimes just by herself to stare at what she could see of the floor through countless tottering legs, roving from exhausting worry to sudden relief whenever Joey left and came back. Who knew how many hours passed? There was no closing time, no curfew, and no agent of family or law wanted to look at how recklessly low the Zimne Piwo Club had gotten on yet another Good Friday night with the annual tantrum of Fat Kuputzniak's melancholy. She tried several times to rearrange and straighten her bra, but couldn't accomplish this without raising her shirt and exposing her breasts. She finally unhooked and pulled the bra all the way off, squeezed it into a ball with both fists, and ditched it under a booth when she was certain nobody was looking.

She was leaning on one of the pool tables, this time with Joey, when Darly Shapinka appeared and asked him how he liked his new little teenage bald pussy. "Does it smell like piss?" she said. "She learn to wipe yet, Joey?"

"I'll take your ass home, goddamn you."

"Will you?" Darly asked, her eyes wide and her hands planted theatrically on her hips in a new manner, affected and beyond her years. "She coming too? Will she suck you like I do?"

"I'll take you goddamn home and make you stay there," Joey said.

Darly moved closer to his face, eyeballing him in a venture of high production. Suzy crept further behind him because Darly was close enough to swing. "You said we don't fuck, Joey. You remember that? You said no matter what we always make love. We make love, you said."

"Give your twat the night off," Joey told her.

Darly held back a sob and spat on the floor, then spread her arms out like a showgirl and sauntered into the middle of the tavern, lifting her shirt and freeing two monstrous, purple breasts that she shook and smacked in a parade that took her through the entire bar, followed by a plastered and fascinated crowd that raised glasses, that clapped and howled, that grabbed at her while she turned now and again to see how Joey would react. He didn't. He lit a cigarette and sucked down two big beers straight in a row.

Suzy was elated by how disgusting Darly Shapinka could make herself look, and the whole scene lifted her from the beaten exhaustion of alcohol and put the glory of warmth and promise back in her spine. She was the winner. Joey had picked *her*. She had succeeded in getting the only man she'd ever wanted. And on the first try. Tonight was just the beginning of her big important life. She would prosper like a bomb that would flatten the Zimne Piwo Club, all the sad little houses built around it, and all the sad losers who lived inside them. They would watch her from the ground as she soared away laughing with Joey Korosa, and she wouldn't feel bad because she'd never have to see any of them ever again.

"I've never had sex," she told Joey. "But I want to with you."

She reached up and kissed him with her tongue. The firm moisture of movement in her mouth triggered a tiny electric memory of Mickey Grogan's tongue, but this was soon erased when Joey crushed her against the bar, grinding his thing into her gut and fumbling with her buttons and her zipper.

"Let's leave," she said. "Not here."

"No," he said. "Here."

They stopped when the roaring in the room suddenly flooded out the noise of the jukebox.

The first thing they saw was Darly. She was completely naked, swinging her shirt over her head, laughing and weeping in the middle of a room that lacked the light and sobriety needed to reveal the veins, stretchmarks, stray black hairs, and pizza grease acne pit scars that crossed and bumped and blemished her skin. Even Fat Kuputzniak came out from behind the bar to get a good horny eyeful, but by then Darly had been pulled away to the men's room, where a line of the drunken and lustful forcefully gathered.

Fat Kuputzniak watched the line, wet-eyed and smiling in a juvenile, oafish way that squeezed the flesh of his face into tight rolls and crammed the bags of his eyes into spectrums of deep gray lines. When the jukebox stopped and the room slightly quieted, Fat Kuputzniak waved his flabby arms in the air and hollered, "Quiet, hold on a second, I gotta say something."

There were covered laughs and somebody told him he should fart whatever he had to say out of his fat ass, but Fat Kuputzniak didn't hear him, and when everyone quieted, he announced in a ridiculous slur, "I wanna thank you for making this goddamn dump a party for once, a real honest-to-shit shakedown . . ."

The jukebox kicked on and cut him off, and he looked around angrily as though this sudden source of noise was a completely mysterious intrusion with the nerve to interrupt him. Then, recognizing his jukebox, he rubbed his hands together and started to dance, a shaking, clapping dance that made everyone laugh. He produced a huge cigar, lit it, and sucked it in his mouth while he clapped and waved to the music. Soon he was drenched in sweat and huffing with fatigue. He went behind the bar to rest and saw a few empty bottles of the nameless white liquor he'd been drinking all afternoon and all night. He gathered the bottles in his arms, the cigar still plugged into his face, then shuffled back onto the floor and tried to juggle them. Everyone ducked. The bottles flew across the room—one, two, three—and exploded against each spot they hit. A framed girly beer poster fell in a clatter of broken glass; a crowded table was cleared of its ashtrays and bottles; the third one missed Mickey Grogan by only an inch. He'd been watching the act from the jukebox, and was showered with glass before he even realized what had happened.

"Shit," he said. "Oh, shit." He instantly considered it another warning from Jesus Christ that he must make contrition for the horrid things he had done and said throughout the years under alcohol's wicked trance. The plant accident had been the first warning. He shot a look at his bandage.

The jukebox quit, and when Fat Kuputzniak tried to gather more bottles, Ape Drape and Coonan and Joey blocked his path and told him to cool his goddamn jets.

"You talk to *me* like that?" he said. "No, no, this is *my* place. I talk to *you*," he said, pointing as stiffly as he could at the youngsters closing in on him, his face a damp gaze of drunken concern. "Goddamn you kids. I talk to you. This is my place and I let you in here and you talk to me like that. I've had enough. Y'understand?"

He blinked and backed away a few steps. His cigar got heavy, and dangled from his face like a spent wet black erection, stretching his lower lip down to show pebbles of greenish teeth planted in septic red gums.

When the cigar finally fell to the floor, he bent forward, reaching, and after wobbling like that over the cigar for a while, he finally fell to the ground and pulled two empty bar stools down with him. The crash was immense, yet Joey and his boys didn't even flinch in an effort to catch him.

"Fat?" Coonan said. "You there, Fat?"

In a moment the music continued, and the boys caught a whiff of horrid odor that rose from the fallen bartender in invisible brown waves.

"Fucking hell," Ape Drape said. "Fat Kuputzniak shit his pants!"

A chant started near the bar that was soon picked up by the rest of the room in a great cheering roar of stomping bottles and glasses and feet that rocked the tavern's walls:

"Fat shit his pants! Fat shit his pants! Fat shit his pants!"

Joey and his friends argued about who would have to take Fat Kuputzniak's legs, but eventually they just dragged him under the shoulders on back to the storage and cooler room behind the bar and propped him up against some boxes.

Suzy was alone for a long time. She sat at the bar and braced herself against the harsh waves of weakness that softened her head with a drunken ache and threatened to cast her from her stool. There were so many people packed inside that the door was propped open and half the party poured onto Pulaski Street. The line for Darly at the men's room had grown to a bacterial cluster from which her voice called in bathroom echoes of cackle and curse among the grunts and cheers from the pile.

Suzy's excitement for the night had been gradually worn down into another heavy sadness, not only by another dark smear of alcohol, but by Joey's sudden sulk at the sight of the line to the toilet. He said nothing, drank, stopped looking at Suzy, stopped touching her. And when she asked him what was wrong, knowing full well what was wrong, yet needing to will him out of caring about anything that happened to Darly, he ignored her. The lift of victory she had felt was gradually buried by seeing how easily Joey disposed of Darly, even though the disposal itself had initially made Suzy elated. She knew well enough that Joey might simply dump her the same way whenever he lost interest, if he had any interest at all. She quietly suffocated from the possibility of being disposed, and she could already feel the jagged anxiety that comes with rejected desires, when hope is dismissed so easily, and there is no chance whatsoever in having the hope fulfilled.

Now Joey was playing bartender with his friends, serving pint glasses of warm liquor straight from the bottles behind the bar and urging everyone to drink them, whether they wanted the drinks or not.

"A beer? Coming right up. But you gotta drink this first."

"What is it?"

"Bourbon and gin and vodka mixed straight."

"No way, it's too much. I'll die. Come on, just give me a beer."

"Don't be a goddamn faggot. Drink up."

And so on. Nobody wanted to be a goddamn faggot. They crowded the bar to get Joey's pint shots, three at a time to take to the kids outside, and over to all the guys waiting for their turn with Darly in the toilet. The pints eventually turned out to be a pretty bad idea; kids were passing out, puking in corners, falling into heaps, crying. Darly yelled out from the toilet a few times, but soon she was laughing again, so nobody made a move to break up the line. The boys who'd gotten their turns stumbled through the tavern, flushed and amazed that something like that could ever happen to any of them, and right there on Pulaski Street. They went outside for air and told the world about Darly Shapinka bent over on the bathroom trashcan, on the sink, the toilet, and Jesus Christ, the stink coming off that girl was like something from the sewer. She was crazy. Only a nutcase would do something like that. Something like that with all those guys at once.

"Figures," someone said. "She had two babies off a nigger, you know."

Then all the kegs ran out. It was hotter than shit in the bar and the whole place smelled like puke. Everyone wanted more beer so they could go outside before the smell made them sick, but when they pulled the taps, only runny foam and air sputtered out. So Joey headed back to the cooler to figure out how to fix them.

Mickey Grogan put five more dollars into the jukebox. He decided that he wouldn't go home that night until he redeemed himself before Suzy Kosasovich, no matter how late he had to stay out, and no matter how worried his mother might get. He knew he didn't have a chance to get any closer to Suzy, to go on a real date with her or anything, and since he'd long given up on that possibility, he only wanted her forgiveness so that he could go to sleep each night without turning in worry at feeling like such a monster. Besides, it was Friday night and there was nothing else to do, and he didn't mind listening to that Bohunk, Crohunk, Polack, and Ukie music anyway. He actually liked it. His drinking buddies from work never did show up that night, and though he had promised his mother that he would not go to the Zimne Piwo Club ever again, he had wanted to see his friends from work and maybe ask them why none of them had visited him in the hospital. And since he wasn't drinking, he didn't consider his presence in the tavern a betrayal to his mother in any way.

He had to get out of that house. He was even thinking about getting out of Joliet. Sitting around all day with his mother was driving him crazy. She kept asking him when he was going back to work, and he hadn't yet told her he'd been fired for drinking on the job. Jesus, even he couldn't believe that one. First his fingers, then his job. And the union, shit. What a rank-and-file crock of shit the goddamn union had been about the whole ordeal. What fucking brotherhood. Cuntluck. Always cuntluck. He figured he'd tell his mother the truth one of these days, but he just didn't know how. God, he hated making her upset, hated making anyone upset, but for some reason he felt like that's all he ever did.

"Hey, bud," somebody said to him. "Pardon me, bud."

There were a few younger boys standing behind him with their arms crossed, and because Mickey thought they wanted a turn at the jukebox, he nervously said, "Oh, sorry, sorry," and stepped aside and vigorously scratched his head.

"We want to know what happened to your hand," the youngest of them said.

Mickey grinned and looked at the floor. He was honored. Blushing. "Aw, guys," he said. "You won't believe this one."

Suzy didn't want to wait for Joey anymore. She was through with waiting around while he slugged around wherever the hell he wanted to and left her by herself. This waiting was starting to make her burn with a grinding, purple rage that made her arms tight and damp with sweat that stuck to the wood on the bar. He was still in the back with the kegs while she was left to wait and fume among the staggering thugs who were waiting for him as well, holding their empty glasses and slurring about when they could get some more goddamn cold beer. They eyed her, rubbed their mouths, and whispered to one another as Darly's baying and panting echoed from the toilet and through the tavern like a hot, moist announcement for free endless flesh and made likely the chance for more. For another piece. For something young like her, like that one sitting there alone and quiet, kind of cute and drunk, and not some crazy, dumpy trashbag whore spitting come through her teeth while a line of cocks waited to plug her like a gas tank.

Suzy heard this talk, knew it was directed at her, and when she heard one of them say, "Tight and clean. Bet she hasn't even been cracked," she slid off the stool and, arms crossed, quickly passed the talk and went behind the bar and quietly pushed herself through the swinging doors and into the storage and cooler to get Joey to take her the hell out of that rotten place for good.

She stopped on the other side of the doors. There was no noise here, the first blanket of silence in hours, hours, and her ears ringing from that silence closed her off from knowing where she really was. This space was dark and littered with boxes and stacks of empty kegs. She felt scared, and didn't know if Joey was even there anymore. She trembled. Maybe Joey had left out some back door, had left to get pills and cocaine and another girl she didn't even know about.

Fat Kuputzniak lay along a wall, flat on his back, with a juicy white arm flung over his eyes. Suzy crept beside him, holding her breath from the stench in his drawers. Then she found the cooler, a steel closet with black rubber tubing around a thick parted door.

She stepped into the cooler and was hit by a gust of freezing air that stung and hardened her nipples, the gust itself smelling like grease and stale beer.

Joey glanced up from the keg he was changing and stared at her through the darkness.

"Joey?" she whispered.

He reached behind her and pulled the door shut, turned on a light, then lifted her onto a stack of beer bottle boxes that felt chilly through the ass of her jeans. He pulled off her shirt and clutched her breasts, bit onto her neck and tasted the chain that hung from it.

"What's that?" he said.

"A relic."

"A what?"

"A relic," Suzy said. "My Busha gave it to me. It's got a piece of Saint Rufina's garments in it."

"Her garments?"

"Her clothes. A piece of her clothes."

"Is it her panties?" he said, pulling her jeans off and palming the warm satin mound between her legs.

She closed her eyes and shivered from the chill and from fright. Beer hissed and pumped from the kegs and up through the plastic tubes than ran along the walls and all the way out to the taps. She tried to kiss him, but his face was in her breasts, then under them, then down to her belly, lower, then lower, until she closed her legs and said, "No, no," fearing she might smell bad down there.

"Have you ever touched come?" Joey asked her. "Have you ever felt a man's come?"

He didn't give her a chance to answer. He was in her that quick, that hard, an exact slicing thrust of pain that made her wince and yelp, and oh, no, she had never touched a man's come, had never seen come, but she was ready to feel Joey's come, ready to rub it in her hands and bring it to her mouth and nose just fresh from him right when he pulled out. She yelped again and said, "Oh, ouch, ouch, you gotta pull it out when you come, Joey, please."

"Goddamnit," he said. "It's so good, it's so fucking good."

He pounded himself steadily, and the pounding hurt her and hurt her, but with the pain, she knew she was giving him such pleasure, such wet pleasure, and she wanted to make him come from the pleasure. She didn't know how much there would be, or what it would look like, yet still she anticipated some flashy, liquid eruption, all hot and sweet and fresh from Joey, from Joey who she finally had alone in some quiet darkness. And bucking on the cold boxes, her relic bouncing against her breasts, the alcohol in her head once again elating her spirits, she reached her arms around him, pulling him to her as close as she could, whispering his name, and as she pulled him tighter, he spastically jerked his head, stiffened as though by cramp, and pushed himself so deeply inside of her that she yelled out, and in her pain she clutched his shoulders just as he released his bolts of sperm far, far inside her. She couldn't feel the come, but knew he hadn't pulled out. Knew it, and there was nothing she could do about it.

He groaned like a cow and made himself laugh as he fell away from her and landed on an empty keg that wobbled under his weight. He pulled his pants up, then found her clothes and gave them to her. "Here," he said.

And that was all. She waited for him to kiss her again, and when he didn't, the temperature of the cooler seized her and she hopped down from the boxes and felt his sperm run chilled down her leg. Like snot in the cold, she thought.

"Joey," she said, and he turned from the cooler door and nodded to hear what she had to say, which was many things at first, then absolutely nothing as she wondered why she had expected anything more, standing there naked and no longer a virgin, dripping and shivering in the romance of tavern storage.

"Come on, get dressed," he said. "Fat Kuputzniak might wake up."

Mickey Grogan's audience had grown and moved from the jukebox to the bar, where Ape Drape and Coonan elbowed each other and smirked and listened to the spastic sketch case babble on about his accident. You'd have though he'd rescued babies from a burning goddamn nursery the way he told it—how he moved around wild-eyed and pointing and waving his arms, brushing his wet red hair away from his face when it fell there in his telling—when everyone knew he'd just fucked up drunk at work and gotten his hand chewed up in a stripper. Like a dumbass. A nigger turned inside out. And now Mickey Grogan wouldn't take a drink, not even a sip, and Coonan wanted to get him wasted, wanted to make him cry, drink his own piss, anything. Anything to stretch the limits of that night's unbelievable and hilarious catastrophes. He and Ape Drape had both taken a turn with Darly, stretched out over the bathroom sink, at the same time, had already busted their rocks while Joey was getting his own slice in the back. Now they were just drunk and bored. Ape Drape liked Coonan's idea of getting Grogan tanked. "Maybe we can get him to shit all over the jukebox," he said.

"Come on, Grogan, drink up," Coonan said. "That's a hell of a story and you deserve a cold one on it. Just one, buddy."

But Mickey wasn't done with his story. "There were doctors all around me up there in the hospital, and they knocked me out with a shot of dope because I wouldn't lay still and stop screaming. I screamed when they took off the towels and I could see all my finger bones, right there," he said, pointing and pointing to the ball of bandage wrapped around his right hand. Nobody gave a shit about the goddamn accident. They were sick of his story, and started walking away and refilling their glasses once the taps started running again.

Coonan and Ape Drape wanted to get much more out of Grogan for having to listen to him at all, so they and a few others hung on and pressed him for more details with their own line of demented questioning.

"Really, Mickey, really," Ape Drape said. "Tell us, and be honest, what did it really feel like? How bad did it hurt?"

Mickey's eyes hardened to prepare for the weight of his answer. He licked his lips and lowered his head in stark reverence to his own suffering. "Bad," he said. "Just like I told you. The worst thing I ever felt, all the skin just ripped right off, bleeding worse than Jesus."

"No, no, not the accident," Ape Drape said. "I mean what did it feel like the first time you took it up the ass?"

Coonan asked Mickey over the laughter if his mother had been there to watch, and if she had provided a cream or a gel to help the fellow in, and Mickey's mind spun from the stress of these questions he knew nothing about, this language of theirs that strangled his own sense of how to tell his own story, since they obviously didn't understand him, and when he tried to go on with it, to tell the rest of it, to elaborate on the process of rehabilitation, the skin on his legs, how his hand had been wrapped and stapled to his leg so the skin on his fingers would grow back just like they were, like new, the others at the bar, guzzling their fresh cold beers, just latched onto the same line of questions that Mickey didn't get.

"What do you think would happen if a guy got his balls caught in a bolt stripper?"

"Yeah, Mickey, what would it do to a guy's balls? What would it do to his cock? Soft or hard? How much blood would there be?"

Mickey scratched his wet red mange, squinting to figure out why they were asking him such things, and willing himself into finishing his story so they would all know what he'd really been through, and how here he was, standing strong enough to tell it.

"What do you think your fingers are gonna look like when they get that bandage off?"

"I told you," Mickey said. "The skin from my leg's growing back on. It's just gonna take some time."

"How much time, Grogan? Weeks? Months?"

"I don't know how long. Maybe a long time."

Groans, shaking heads, downturned eyes, sad, sad sounds of pitiful disbelief from them all.

"Jesus, Mickey, you might have that big goddamn wrap on your hand for the rest of your life."

"I don't get it, Grogan. How's that work? Leg skin, finger skin, hand skin. It don't add up. I think that doctor's just pulling your sack so you won't feel bad."

Mickey shook his head and said, "No, no, no," and wished the doctor was there right now to tell them all just like he'd told him. The fingers will look like new, he had said. A common procedure.

"I bet your fingers are gonna look like some old broad's rotten twat."

"Hey, yeah, the same thing happened to my uncle. When they unwrapped him his fingers looked so bad and fucked up they had to cut off his whole goddamn hand. No bullshit. Right at the wrist."

"Nobody's cutting my hand off," Mickey argued. "No goddamn way, man. The doctor told me—"

"Believe what you want to, Grogan."

"Maybe you'll catch a sixty-to-one trifecta at Balmoral and buy yourself a whole new hand. You know, one of those plastic or wooden deals that cripples and war vets wear."

"I won't need a new hand!" Mickey hollered, and Ape Drape broke into a drawn wheeze of laughter that infuriated Mickey into a state of argument he wasn't used to employing. His lip inadvertently trembled and his hands shook. "You'll see!" he said. "Ha ha! We'll see who's laughing then, man."

"Let's see right now!" Coonan told him. "Let's see how your great goddamn doctor's work is coming along."

"See what?" Mickey said.

"The hand," Coonan told him. "Come on, go ahead, let's get a good look at that hand. We want to see your doctor's fine work."

"But it's all wrapped up. And it's gotta stay wrapped up."

"Just unwrap it then. Give us a look!"

"A preview!"

"Aw, no way, hey," Mickey said. "I don't think that's a good idea. The doctor said—"

"Fuck the doctor," Ape Drape told him. "Is it the goddamn doctor's hand or your hand? Whose fingers are fucked here, Grogan? Come on!"

"All you gotta do is wrap it back up," Coonan Said. "We'll even help you."

"I don't know."

"Yes, you know!"

"Come on, Mickey!"

"Unwrap that fucker! For yourself. For your peace of mind."

Mickey wondered if they were right. Maybe the doctor was just fooling with him so he wouldn't feel bad. He decided in a flash to unwrap it. For himself. For his own peace of mind. He was about to mightily, proudly declare that he was going to just go ahead and do it, knowing their excitement and suspense would return in a glorious tribute of applauded respect for his bravery, when something happened that took his audience's attention completely away from him.

Darly Shapinka stumbled out of the men's room, slapping at the handful of guys who were still waiting there for her. She was naked, wet, and her hair hung over her eyes in clumps and strands. Nobody had ever seen Darly Shapinka's hair in that state, fallen drenched from the tight tail she always kept it in, and to see her like that, Christ, to see Darly Shapinka looking like that, even the few who hadn't gotten a turn at her no longer wanted to. Their hard-ons sank and shriveled the moment she emerged from the toilet. Her tits sagged like wheat sacks and swung heavily as she gathered her clothes from the places she had dropped them and awkwardly pulled them back on. The jukebox was silent between songs and everybody watched her, the sickest creature on Pulaski Street. In her gathering she found a rumpled bra under a booth, and picking it up, she remembered that she had not put on a bra that day. She shot her eyes up to scan the room for Joey and Suzy, and when she didn't see them, she instantly knew goddamn well who the bra belonged to. She saw instead the many staring and awe-sickened faces and said, "Oh, fuck off. All of you. Go fuck yourself where you eat."

She chased this down with an abandoned half-pint of some obscure brown liquor taken from a nearby table, sucked it down in three firm gulps, then coughed and spat and wiped off her mouth with the back of her hand. Then she sat at the table alone and combed and tied her hair back into the tight tail the way it was supposed to be. She looked at nobody, sneered at nobody, just expertly combed her hair and tied it back and sat by herself, and fuck Joey and the rest of them anyway. The jukebox was back on and eventually everyone in the bar stopped watching her, since there was nothing left to watch, nothing compared to seeing her naked and stumbling from the toilet to find her clothes, and soon she was quietly overlooked and left for a dumb, drunk whore whose service was no longer needed.

When she was satisfied with the way her hair was restored, she leaned back in the chair and thought about what would happen next with Joey. This wasn't over. They weren't over. He was probably gone for now with that little bitch from the bus somewhere. She didn't care about where they'd gone or how they were fucking, since they'd only met that night. It wasn't real. Darly knew it was she, and not that little bald pussy, who Joey made love to. Didn't fuck, but made love to. He told her that all the time and she believed it, and how many times over how many years had they made love?

The only person Darly Shapinka hated as much as Suzy Kosasovich was herself. And in the toilet, bent over the trashcan, stretched over the sink, she had given herself a beating that had at first been a little fun, that had felt good in both practice and, more importantly, principle—the principle of showing Joey he wasn't the only guy she could get, and Jesus Christ, did she get a lot of them that night, and the principle of showing him how she could turn on her heel and do her own goddamn thing, whatever the hell she wanted when he tossed her away for the night, for some young bald piece that wanted and took him. Darly knew that Joey had hated seeing that line to get her, young new piece or not, just hated seeing those guys lining up for her. And wasn't that the point? Oh, but it was bad, bad after all. Sure, she'd fucked tons of guys, sucked off even more, but she'd never done anything like that. Not all at once in front of everybody like that. In the toilet, after a while, the acts had long ago gone beyond her own doing. She was taken and probed and stuck and worked on like a junk car a bunch of guys wanted to gear up and run. She'd been roughed and flattened, had permitted them to rough and flatten her, and that, she figured, was what you do when you hate yourself more than anyone else. More than anyone else except that little bald bitch from the bus.

She'd warned her to back off. The girl hadn't listened, and since Darly had given herself her own sort of beating that night, for Joey and for herself and for anyone else who might have thought her weak and clinging to a guy who'd tossed her off in front of the whole goddamn tavern when he'd said, goddamn him, when he'd told her to give her twat the night off, now it was time for that bitch from the bus. Because she had warned her. She shouldn't have warned her, should have just beat her ass early on before Joey had a chance to like getting chased and wanted by someone new and young. She, Darly, might have hated herself, but she'd never moved in on another girl's man right in front of her, mocking her and laughing at her like that. That little bitch was awfully young, but to hell with whether she knew better or not. She would beat her ass red. Who knew where she and Joey had gone? But it would happen. It didn't matter when. She'd beat her ass red and right down in front of everyone, just to show them, just to let them know that she and Joey weren't over. She'd get her, street, store, bus, she'd give her a good Queen Darly Shapinka beating that would bend and age her face at least three years.

Coonan brought Darly a shot. "Wild night, baby," he said.

"Did you like it?"

"Oh, goddamn hell I liked it. I knew I would."

"You seen Joey?"

"He's in back changing the kegs," Coonan said. "They ran out. We drank all of Fat Kuputzniak's goddamn beer," he said, and laughed, then went back to the bar to get another one for himself.

Suzy wished she'd kept her bra. The storage room was too cold, even standing outside of the cooler near Fat Kuputzniak, shivering and holding her nose from his stink. There was nowhere else to stand. He'd rolled over and sprawled himself entirely over the storage walkway. And he was snoring. She had to stand there because she was once again waiting for Joey, who was pissing in a garbage tub back in the corner. She wanted to take a deep breath for warmth, but the steady gurgle of snoring and the splash of urine against the plastic tub sounded through the cluttered darkness and kept her fingers pinched firmly on her nose. When she tried to inhale through her mouth, her throat swelled with involuntary disgust and she gagged so hard tears came to her eyes.

The relic felt like a chain of ice between her breasts, but when she thought about taking it off and sticking it in her pocket, she got superstitious, shivering from the thought of losing its protection. Not Saint Rufina's, Busha's, or anyone else's, but the protection of the relic itself, the magic piece of cloth inside the circle of glass. A holy good luck charm. It had protected her from Darly Shapinka, had gotten her Joey, and had gotten him to fuck her, yes, not at all the way she had wanted him to, but the night wasn't over, or maybe this was just how Joey liked to do it. Maybe this was how everyone did it. How could she know?

When Joey was finished, he took her arm and slowly led her over and past Fat Kuputzniak and toward the swing doors back into the tavern, and in taking her arm like that, Suzy knew there would be more of Joey Korosa to look forward to.

They were back in the acrid tavern, in all the smoke and polka music. But she didn't care where they were, didn't care about what a puke-smelling dump of a place this was, because Joey hadn't pulled out. She could still feel him wet between her legs, and every-one saw them come out together, she and Joey, and she knew they could all tell she and Joey had just done it, and Jesus, was she proud they all knew it, and Joey's friends all nodded and grinned, and there was Mickey Grogan at the bar, watching them come out to-gether, and then through the smoke and puke-smell and the grin-ning, nodding friends, came Darly, clothed again, charging right for Suzy, screaming through her teeth, louder the closer she got, screaming through her bent mouth and teeth, "You goddamn whore, you man-stealing cunt." She grabbed the front of Suzy's shirt, pulled her to the ground, and began pounding the top of her head, still screaming, "You whore, you bald-pussied cunt, you man-stealer," her fist a weighted rubber hammer striking and striking Suzy's skull, and Suzy screamed for help, "Help me, oh God, God help me," and then she screamed no words, just screamed, cover-ing herself and cowering under the blows, but no matter how hard she'd scream or try to cover herself, Darly's fist got through to pound and pound, and there was no sound or smell or smoke to re-gard, no sensation of Joey and his sperm inside of her, just an ex-cruciating ringing blur of Darly's fist against her head. Then Darly ripped the relic off and, squeezing it in her fist, beat the side of Suzy's face—her cheek, her temple—and still, no matter how hard she screamed and tried to cover herself, bent and curled in a ball on the floor, Darly's fist got through and struck and beat Suzy until she went limp and half blacked out.

Joey finally wrapped his arms around Darly and pulled her off. He was laughing. Darly kicked in his arms as he carried her across the room and dumped her by the door. Suzy had somehow ended up on the wet floor behind the bar, and she lay there sobbing and clutching her head, so she did not see Joey and Coonan hold Darly back when she tried to push past them, still yelling about what a man-stealing cunt-of-a-whore that bald-pussied bus bitch was, and she did not see the boys push Darly outside and slam and lock the door behind her, first laughing, then ducking, when Darly pitched a bottle through the front door's small square of black painted glass.

Joey had forgotten all about Suzy, had completely stopped thinking about her while he and Coonan pressed themselves against the door. They were howling about the busted glass, and about Darly ramming herself against the other side of the door, rocking and jolting it, and yelling through the window, "Open the goddamn door you cocksuckers!" Her face filled the space where the black glass used to be, her whole red furious pan of a face spitting through the empty square, her eyes and veins bulging. Then she was gone.

"She went to get gasoline," Coonan said. "She's going to pour gasoline down the chimney."

"She's going to cut my balls off, man," Joey said. "She's going to cut off my balls and bake them and serve them to me at her own kitchen table. She knows how to cook. Whenever we fuck she cooks for me after. I've been real bad to her tonight. I said the ugliest things to her I've ever said. And then balling that girl in the back with Darly right out here. In the same place." A sad and heavy drag from too much booze—The Guilties, he and his friends called it— suddenly recollected in him a distorted devotion to Darly Shapinka and obliterated his ceaseless claim that he wasn't her boyfriend, that he wasn't anybody's goddamn boyfriend. "Darly's been my steady fuck for three years. That's hard shit, Coonan."

Coonan saw that he was slipping into a sadness that might very well put an end to the night, and Christ, the night wasn't anywhere near over as far as he was concerned. "Steady fuck my ass, Korosa. You ball any quim that comes along and you know it. Darly's a whore."

"Fuck you, Coonan. She's no whore."

"Sorry. No, she's not a whore. Sorry."

"Did you do her in the toilet? Did you and Ape Drape do her in the toilet with the rest of them? I wouldn't be too mad if you did. Did you?"

"Hell no, Korosa. Come on. Get some piss in you. You're our fuck artist, Joey. The fuck artist of Pulaski Street. You've got your own fuck museum down the block. Forget about it. Let's just have a good goddamn time."

"Fuck artist," Joey said musingly.

They were laughing again, laughing so hard they had to wipe their eyes like a couple of old women. Christ, did Joey want a drink. "I'm the one who changed the goddamn kegs!" he yelled, and Coonan threw his arm around him and they unlocked and unblocked and wandered away from the door and to the bar, stepping over and crunching the broken bottle and window glass spread all over the floor.

Mickey Grogan had not forgotten about Suzy. He had desperately tried to save her from Darly, but hadn't been able to get through the cheering huddle that surrounded her. What a perfect redemption that would have been for him. To have lifted her from the beating with his one good hand, to have pried himself through that crazy, cheering huddle, and to have lifted and carried her to safety with his one good hand. She would have forgiven him, thought him a friend instead of a monster. And the rest of them would have seen the strength of his good hand, and what the bad hand and the bad fingers looked like wouldn't have mattered anymore. They'd have left him alone about the bandage, and he wouldn't have been expected to take it off. But none of that had happened, and now he'd have to take the bandage off and show them. Shit, he could have done it, could have gotten right in there and lifted her away from that beating with his good hand and with his good hand alone. And with his good hand he had squeezed and pushed wildly, trying to get through the huddle, had pushed and pried, pushed and pried. But there were too many bigger people hustling for a space to watch the beating, and they shoved him away. And as many more rushed in from outside, he was shoved straight back into the huddle and shouldered aside. And in that fury of shoving Mickey heard Suzy screaming for help, and in his last attempt to get through to her he fell down right in the middle of the crowd and landed on his bad hand and cried out. He pulled himself up and scurried away, having given up on the idea of saving anyone but himself.

Then Joey Korosa pulled Darly out of there and the huddle split and spread to see what would happen next, leaving Suzy knocked out on the floor, still crooked and curled, clutching her head in her arms. Mickey hurried and knelt down to her, gently lifted her head and legs to get her sitting up straight. She opened her eyes and saw Mickey, not Joey, lifting her up and trying to help, the only person in the whole damn bar who wanted to help her (and she knew why he wanted to help her, the degenerate), and he was touching her head and her legs, and his bandage stank of something wet and bodily, an oily sweat on dirty skin, goddamn him, goddamn his nasty red hair, and she slapped him away and crawled off to the sodden floor behind the bar and lay there and wept.

Mickey didn't know what to do. He carefully, deferentially followed her behind the bar, knelt, asked if he could see her face, tried to give her some ice wrapped up in a towel in case there was swelling, but all she said was, "No, just leave me alone, just get the fuck away from me," shaking, and crying into her arms. Mickey stood there for a moment behind the bar, stood there over her with his hands on his hips in a display of authority and concern. Nobody else was checking on her. They glanced at her there on the floor without scrutiny or care, since there were many, many others curled and unconscious in random spaces throughout the tavern. In corners, under tables, flat on their backs by the toilet, some next to puddles of their own bright vomit.

"Hey, Suzy," Mickey said. "How about a glass of water? You want to go to the bathroom?"

She ignored him. He still didn't know what to do. And then Mickey Grogan, hands still dignifiedly resting on his hips, was suddenly, guiltlessly gathered into the urge to take and drink from the many bottles that lined the shelves before him. So he did. A fresh bottle of J&B. An empty tumbler. Three deep shots right in a row. He drank them and he didn't care. He drank them and took the bottle and the tumbler to the end of the bar and offered to share them with the guys who wanted to see him take his bandage off.

"Grogan, Grogan, you're catching up, old chap," Coonan told him.

"Here here!" said Ape Drape.

"Back on the hooch, Mickey. Better stay away from the jukebox or else you'll get your other hand chewed up in the gears, you monkey-assed pussylover."

Within minutes the bottle he'd brought over was empty. The rush of liquor shot up and down his spine in waves that spread to his heart and his head like a zealot communicant's first taste of the transubstantiated wine of Christ's precious blood, and glowingly prepared him for his next proclamation:

"Awright, goddamnit, I'm taking this bandage off in two more drinks! You hear me? Two more drinks!"

"Goddamn right, Grogan!"

"Take it off!"

They cheered, clapped, cleared some space, poured him shots, and raised their glasses once again for yet another promise of some poor fucked-over loser's willing and voluntary spectacle.

By then, after a long awful time on the beer-drenched rubber slab behind the bar, after crying, weakening from crying even more than she already was, sniffling, flinching from spasms of lost breath, Suzy Kosasovich clutched the bar sink with both hands and slowly pulled herself to stand. Pain rushed sharply to her head, and she grabbed back onto the sink to stop herself from falling over. The entire right side of her face throbbed outward in a tight, spreading swell. And she was drenched in beer all up and down the front of her shirt and her jeans. She saw Joey drinking and laughing down at the end of the bar with a group that included Mickey Grogan, and at once she was startled into believing that Joey and Mickey and the rest of them were all part of some obscene thug conspiracy set to fuck up and mutilate her into the dirt. But when she saw that Mickey Grogan was drunk again, wavering and happy in the middle of the guys despite their sidelong smirks and exclusive laughter, Suzy discounted the fear as traumatized paranoia.

She waited for Joey to turn his head and notice her standing there straight and having survived, to notice her risen and strong enough to have endured that kind of beating, and all for him, just for him. But he didn't see her, so she quietly stumbled away to the toilet.

There were a few sick and sleeping girls on the ladies' room floor that Suzy had to step over to get to the mirror. She didn't blame Joey for forgetting about her behind the bar. Her mascara had run and smeared down her face in lines like black cracks, and the beaten side of her face was yellowing around the aching swell. She wanted to cry again, but her eyes were so dry and tight and exhausted from sobbing that she simply couldn't. Her lip quivered, but there was not one solid whimper left in her. Her face strained in the effort, but the result was just a sort of sullen dry heave behind the eyes.

She rinsed the smears from her face and tried to gather some hope for what was left of the night. At least Joey had saved her from Darly. Maybe he didn't know where she had gone. Maybe he thought she had just left the tavern, and was drinking in that group to forget about how horrible he felt for letting her slip away all beaten and ashamed. Maybe that was the reason. After all, Darly Shapinka was gone, gone, gone, and Suzy wasn't. She was still here in the Zimne Piwo Club and Joey hadn't kicked her out. She forced herself to feel what was left of the wet warmth of Joey's kiss, and she urged the sensation back through the throbbing that pulsed in the places where Darly had struck her. The fresh memory of Joey's mouth almost caused her to forget about the pain, almost restored the possibility of a joyful conclusion to her longing. He would kiss her again.

She was holding herself up on the bathroom sink, and when she opened her eyes she was disgusted anew with her own face, even without the smeared makeup, and then she felt lashed with a hysterical panic. Her relic was missing. She bolted for the door and back into the bar to find it, and in doing so she stepped right on a sleeping girl's hand and the girl woke and sat up and yelled, "Ow, ow, fuck you, fuck you!" but Suzy was already gone.

Suzy flung herself through the door and ran smack into a wall of sweat-drenched bodies that had piled into the bar to a dangerously tight capacity. She could not see the other end of the room through the mass. It was the most packed the tavern had gotten that night, and, for that matter, the most loaded the Zimne Piwo Club had been in its forty-some years of operation. Something else had happened in the time she had spent in the ladies' room, and whatever had happened was still happening, and everyone and more had poured in off the street to see it. Tables and chairs had been pushed away to the edges of the room, and as Suzy edged her way around the crowd, she saw that the crowd had assembled in a cheering circle to surround what she figured was another fight. Whatever it was they were surrounding, the massed rabble made it impossible to try to find her relic. She tried but could not get close to the spot where Darly had ripped it from her and, she hoped, had dropped it somewhere kicking away in Joey's arms.

Squeezing through the bodies, she tried to find Joey, and as she did she saw what the horde had gathered around to see: Mickey Grogan standing on a chair in the middle of the circle, his bandaged hand held high in a manner of grand presentation. In his other hand was a tumbler double shot. He was red-eyed, swollen, rambling again, specks of spit like weak sparks from a busted engine popping from his wet lips. Nobody could, nor needed to, hear what he had to say, and soon he clumsily downed the double shot and coughed some of it back up and slapped away the strand of drool that swung from his chin with his good hand, dropped the empty glass to the floor, then tottered, wide-eyed, with his arms outstretched, in a near-fall from the chair, a fall the crowd would sure have loved to see. Then he steadied himself and unlatched the metal clasps that held the bandage closed, peeled open the end of the strand, and began to unwrap it.

"Take it off, Grogan!"

"Pull that fucker loose, Mickey!"

Suzy hated the whole idea of watching anything that involved a widely applauded demonstration starring Mickey Grogan, even if he was at that moment unknowingly the subject of an over-whelmingly shared ridicule. But an angrier part of her imagination wanted to see his hand, the selfsame hand that had violated her in her own younger naiveté, the hand now all gnarled and sickening. Then she spotted Joey and remembered her relic, and went to him and asked him if he had seen it.

"Your what?"

"My Saint Rufina relic."

"Saint Ra-who-who?" he said, breaking into laughter and re-turning his attention to Mickey Gorgan's ceremonious exposition on the chair in the middle of the room. Suzy forced herself to be-lieve that Joey wasn't being cruel, but instead teasing her just as he had when they'd first met that night, squeezed together at the bar, smoking cigarettes together and flirting. She remembered that mo-ment and clung to it and directed it to explain to herself the mean way Joey was acting. But she couldn't convince herself to believe that entirely.

"Go on, Grogan!" Joey yelled through the amplifier of his cupped hands.

"Can you please help me find it, Joey? We could go somewhere else, then. We could go down to the canal, and we could do it again, too."

"Oh sure, sure, baby," he said, slinging his arm around her and sort of pulling her close to him, and though his eyes were slack and blood-pocked in the corners, and though his words were slurred,

Suzy believed him entirely. She waited right by his side, even after he took his arm away from her to whistle with his fingers and clap for Mickey, who was working faster on his rickety stage, turning away the long strand from his hand and letting it gather in a pile at his feet until it finally spilled over the side of the chair and onto the floor while the audience cheered and whistled for him to go on.

The ball had gotten much smaller, and when Mickey recognized how close he was to seeing what was under it, he paused and apprehensively looked down at the piled stand of bandage he had already removed. He was in the midst of changing his mind about the whole performance when he glanced up and saw how many people were watching him, the whole loaded tavern staring at him and clamoring voraciously to see his hand.

"Goddamn, Grogan, don't stop now!"

And God, he'd gotten drunk again. He wanted to stop it all, wrap his hand back up and just quit. Just go home. But he was drunk. Bad drunk. And his mother would be waiting up for him, and he had no job, and his friends from work hadn't shown up, and there were so many people staring and cheering and clapping at him that soon the thought of running away seemed equally as awful as staying. He tried to turn his back to the crowd, making careful steps on what little space there was to the seat of the chair, but he was surrounded in every direction. When he turned back around, he wasn't as careful on his feet and the chair gave and wobbled, and he stooped and thrust his arms out to stop himself from falling. He was sure they would all laugh, but their response was instead a suddenly queer and quiet retreat of whispers and muted groans, and it wasn't until Mickey Grogan stood straight again and opened his eyes when he saw that the rest of the bandage had fallen away. What was left of his bad hand was a disaster: a glove of pink ground beef for fingers and raw wet chicken for the rest. It glistened, the air brought it great pain, and in the middle of that stilled moment of sickened gawking, Suzy regretted having wanted to look at Mickey Grogan's bad hand at all. She was thankful that at least she hadn't wished such an affliction upon him, no matter what he had done the summer before. Poor Mickey, she let herself think. Poor, poor Mickey Grogan. Her disgust at Mickey vanished suddenly, and was replenished with a tender memory of the grade-school child Mickey Grogan, two years too old for fifth grade, his face stupid and naked with shame, cowering in his desk under a reddened and bellowing Sister Innocenta from Saint Cyril's Elementary admonishing him for passing gas too loudly instead of holding it in until he got his turn for the lavatory.

Joey Korosa whistled through his teeth, then said, "That is the most disgusting fucking thing I have ever seen in my whole life."

Mickey made a face and hid his bad hand in his jacket. He stepped off of the chair for his bandage, shivering and gasping, but Ape Drape had snatched it away when Mickey wasn't looking, had wrapped it back up into a big, tight ball and, smiling, tossed it over Mickey's head, where Coonan was waiting to catch it.

"Come on!" Mickey begged. "Don't do that!"

A round of keep-away began, Mickey in the middle, darting from person to person as his bandage soared over his head. He reached with both hands to unsuccessfully catch it, and when everyone got another good look at the horrid hand, pink and yellow and glistening, they groaned and moved away from him as though to stop the spread of whatever infected disease had set in the raw skin. Which made Mickey all the more desperate in his pursuit, and the tossers all the more nimble in their strategic resistance to his attempts.

"I need that back!" he pleaded. "Please, guys, please give it back!"

"Let it breathe for a while, Grogan. Dig fast!"

Suzy was scanning the floor for her relic, and when she saw no sign of it, she went back to Joey and said, "Please help me find it. Please. My Busha gave it to me and I don't know what she'll do if I lose it. Please. Then we can go do it again if you want. We can go somewhere to be alone."

"Sure, sure, but not right yet," he told her. "I've just gotta watch this shit. Look at that fucker's hand." Joey caught the bandage then, held it as high as his long arm would stretch, and Mickey Grogan ran to him, pleading and pleading to have it back, holding his bad hand close to his chest, heavy tears now falling from his eyes. "It hurts bad, Joey," he said. "Please give it back to me."

"Just let him have it," Suzy said, in part to put an end to Mickey's pain, but mostly to put an end to the whole event so that Joey would help her find her relic and then leave with her to be alone.

Joey ignored them both and tossed the bandage away, and a few younger guys backstepped, struggling to catch the ball like drunken wedding reception bachelors chasing the bride's stolen garter.

Suzy scattered through the room, squinting in the dim light for a sign of the chain and the glass circle, then behind the bar, and from that spot she watched two boys reach their limit of having to listen to that stupid fucking polka jukebox. Together they picked up a bar stool on both sides and ran it across the room, right through the keep-away ring—past Joey, Ape Drape, Coonan, past darting, reaching Mickey Grogan—and as a battering ram they propelled the bar stool straight into the jukebox. Once for the growl of needle scratch that crackled and punctured the speakers. Twice to smash the glass on the display, chunks of black record plastic flying into the air from the electric burst within, then three, four, and five more times to completely destroy it. They left the machine impaled by the bar stool, legs out, spitting sparks and small flames, then smoldering with black smoke that smelled of melted album vinyl and ozone. The outlet behind the machine flashed in a brief succession of white strobes, buzzed with an over-loaded short that dimmed all the lights in the bar a few times before it finally gave up its power and died. Quarters spilled from the side of the jukebox, and yet another crowd rushed over to collect them. This inspired others to plunder the entirety of the Zimne Piwo Club. They hustled past Suzy behind the bar and tried to open the cash register, and when they couldn't figure it out, they picked it up and brought it out to Pulaski Street, dropped it onto the asphalt with a crash, then grabbed all the money inside. Five, tens, twen-ties, and all the coins. Inside, a trio of boys considered grabbing the television set that hung on the wall behind the bar.

"What the fuck for? It's an old black-and-white chunk of dog-shit," one said.

So a deranged, cackling, acne-faced boy with long yellow hair hurled a full pint glass at the blank television screen, creating a mas-sive burst and a shower of beer and shattered glass from the gaping void of the busted set left to look like a mouth widely screaming from torture.

They grabbed bottles of liquor behind the bar, while others headed back to the storage and hurriedly lifted whole boxes of booze and cases of beer and fresh cold kegs and rolled them out onto the street, then down to the alleys, garages, and basements in and around Pulaski Street, fuel for countless parties that would flare on until dawn.

Suzy was gradually giving up any hope of finding the relic, and replacing that hope with the hope of at least getting Joey alone down by the barge canal. She returned again and again to the memory of the moment they'd first spoken. Tucked so closely be-side him at the bar, she could smell his fresh, clean sweat despite the fumes of booze and cigarette smoke, spilled beer pooled slop-pily into rank black ashtrays. Now he was still running the keep-away circle, and Mickey Grogan was sobbing for his bandage, hold-ing his bad hand in his jacket and bawling, "It hurts, it hurts, give it back, come on!"

"Woo-hoo, Grogan! Come and get it! Come get your nasty-ass wrap!"

As more kegs were rolled out of the cooler and storage, Fat Kuputzniak was violently stirred awake. He sat up and watched for an inadvertently long while as the young emptied his walk-in cooler. And though the young saw that he was awake, they did not drop their loot and run, but instead tried to be a little quicker, more efficient.

"He's up, move your ass, get that case, and you, get that keg."

"He really up? His eyes are open, but do you think he's really awake?"

"Who gives a fuck? Come on, move."

They, the young, were emptying and emptying his business, and Fat Kuputzniak sat there and watched them do it, feebly drunk, still half-asleep and only nebulously aware of how blatantly and exces-sively disrespectful this emptying actually was.

Then it hit him, slid through his soft semi-consciousness power-fully enough to make him call out, "You all stop! Put that back right goddamn now!" Then he erupted into an extensive coughing fit that jostled his shoulders like a dump truck over potholes. By the time the coughing stopped there was nobody emptying his cooler for him to chase and beat, children they were be damned, to chase and beat the way any good liquor-sick drunk deserved to do when

74

his livelihood was threatened. He stood and felt the wet hunk of load in his pants and said, "Oh, Lord. King Christ on His throne." He'd shat his bed a few times after blackout benders at closing with some of the other barkeeps he knew from that side of town. But this shitting himself during business hours was a terribly shameful first, and when he thought of his dead kid sister looking down at him from Heaven, he crossed himself and said in his head, *I'm sorry, Mary. I gotta drink so much because I still miss you so bad. You've been dead thirty years and I'm a drunken mess and I soiled my pants, and I'm sorry.*

He thought then about the way her body had flailed loosely through the clear blue air when she'd been hit. They'd been walking home together from Good Friday services at Saint Cyril's. From Veneration of the Cross. A friend had called out to her from across the street, and Mary hadn't looked before she ran to meet her. The car had kicked her way into the air, her arms and legs flailing puppet-like. He had watched her sail through the air from the sidewalk, just standing on the sidewalk, his hands over his mouth, and the sound her head made when it hit the street half a block ahead—a clap, a flat asphalt crack of a clap—was the ugliest sound he'd ever heard, because it had immediately made it clear to him that Mary was already dead. They buried her in her white communion dress, in a white casket, and with a strand of white rosary beads interlaced through her small folded hands.

She died on Good Friday just like Jesus Christ, the priest had said at her burial mass. And so like Christ and a child of Christ, Mary Kuputzniak would ascend directly to the Kingdom of Heaven. This had infuriated Fat Kuputzniak. He and his sister had been in the same church only a few days before, and now they were back, but she was in a casket, and if it hadn't been for church, for Good Friday, they would have just stayed at home together and she wouldn't have gotten killed. So as the priest extolled the virtues of young Mary Kuputzniak, promised the mourners that the Kingdom had already received her newly reposed soul, Fat Kuputzniak, who was then only seventeen-year-old Artie Kuputzniak, had glared at the priest from the front pew and thought, *You frocked faggot.*

He steadied his walk out of the storage by bracing his hands against the narrow walkway walls, following the riot of voices he heard on the other side of the swing doors. But where was the music? The mess in his pants made him waddle like a toddler with a loaded diaper through the doors and back into the tavern, and when he saw what was left of the place, the broken glass, the bodies, the vomit, the overturned tables and chairs, the barspace sparse without bottles or cash register, and finally the jukebox, crushed and impaled and smoldering in the middle of the room, Fat Kuputzniak roared, "Oh, Lord! Lord!" and, for the first time in thirty years, covered his mouth with his hands.

The room fell still and silent. Afraid. The bartender's eyes were smaller, puffy, red with clogged tears. A pair of moist sores.

"My kid sister's been dead thirty years!" he bellowed. "You're my guests tonight, and I let you all in because you're kids like she was, and goddamn all of you for what you done to my place! Where's all my liquor? Where's my goddamn cash register? And what in the fuck did you do to my jukebox?" He went behind the bar and came up with the blunt end of a pool cue wrapped in black rubber tape. He clutched it in his fists and made a move to waddle into the room to clear everybody out with it. Within a few steps two boys came out of the back with an empty refrigerator-sized cardboard packing box that they lifted and crammed over the bartender, pulling it over him completely with a great struggle that marked Fat Kuputzniak's last attempt at resistance. They spun the box and spun the box and then the box tottered on its own, emitting from within it a muffled storm of curses, colliding into people who shoved it away in a comical romp that sent the box reeling into barstools, walls, a few chairs. Fat Kuputzniak was blinded and trapped. His arms were pressed to his sides inside the box so that he could not free himself from it no matter how much force he thrust forth from his girth. The top of the box was flat against his head. The black, blunt pool cue dropped from the bottom like, someone remarked, another Kuputzniak shitlog. "Goddamn, Fat, we're gonna have to build you an outhouse on wheels!" And someone grabbed the black pool cue and playfully rapped the top and sides of the box, which was still spinning, colliding, and cursing.

And the keep-away game resumed as the staggering box made for an impromptu obstacle to keep Mickey from getting his bandage back. Now Mickey and the box were both surrounded. Pushed, teased, kept from, tossed over. Slamming into each other. Everyone laughing. Sweet Jesus Christ. Look at this place. Look at Fat all trapped up, that fuck. Look at Mickey Grogan's sick-ass hand. Until the box eventually became a rank shit-smelling annoyance that Coonan got rid of by grabbing the black cue and mercilessly beating the sides of the box, then slamming the top with all of his Kuluzni Brothers lard-packing might. The box moaned with a gurgling howl, and blood spurted from a split at the top, and the box slowly turned and stumbled, dragging one leg behind, until it finally crashed across the broken plastic and glass next to the smoldering jukebox, a fresh puddle of urine spreading from a dark, growing stain on the bottom of the cardboard.

"Jesus, Coonan, you killed him!"

"Nah, he ain't dead. Look, he's still pissing," Coonan said, then braced the cue like a baseball bat and smacked the pitched ball of bandage clear across the room.

※

The relic was gone. Or, if not gone, impossibly lost in the cluttered filth of broken glass and the scum of spilled alcohol smeared across every inch of the Zimne Piwo Club. Suzy couldn't look for it anymore. Her back ached from bending, as did her eyes from squinting and straining in the barlight, which seemed even dimmer now above the soft noise of occasional and exhausted talk among the remaining few who had stayed behind to sprawl out among some stools and chairs in the tired quiet of the tavern. The kegs were running low and, since there were none left in the storage cooler to replace them, what little talk there was concerned where to go next. So and so's basement. That guy's garage. Alley. Backyard.

The fallen, bloodstained, piss-soaked cardboard box of Fat Kuputzniak made a noise and stirred, which, somebody muttered, was "utterly fucking hysterical."

"See?" Coonan said. "Alive and kicking. A fat sack of living, kicking shit. I didn't kill anyone."

"What about the canal?" someone asked.

"Aw, fuck the canal. Not tonight," said Ape Drape.

"How come?"

"Because whatever's happening ain't happening down there."

Which was fine with Suzy, who needed the benches along the canal empty and to herself so that she and Joey could finally have a dark and quiet privacy where nothing was happening in the next room to take Joey's attention away. She was sitting apart from the others and waiting for the game of keep-away to end. The running and throwing had gradually stopped, though Mickey Grogan still didn't have his bandage. He stood, no longer crying, his bad hand still hidden away under his jacket, his eyes pink and half-lidded, waiting for somebody to give it back. The sprawled—Joey, Coonan, Ape Drape, and three or four more—had worn themselves out in the match, and sat there, all of them grinning and beat, no way in hell anywhere even near ready to give the bandage back after a roll like that, Coonan holding it in a fist under lazily crossed arms. Suzy wanted to grab the bandage from him and hand it to Mickey herself. Making him stand there and beg was a whole new kind of bad, bad low, and she hated having to sit there and watch it. Again she saw in Mickey's face the fifth grader two years too old. Passing gas and all the kids laughing at him not only because of the gas but because they all knew, as the whole school knew, that Mickey Grogan was too stupid to be in seventh grade. Little kids laughing at him, Sister Innocenta scolding. Then he had asked for the restroom, but he mispronounced and called it the laboratory, and then even Sister Innocenta laughed at him, called him a stupid, stupid boy before she sent him out of the room with a wave and hopelessly condescending shake of her black-hooded head. Suzy wanted to grab the bandage from Coonan, wanted to present it to Mickey so he could finally leave the place with his pride, but she didn't have the courage to face the ridicule and anger from Joey and his friends that such an action would provoke, to break up the game and the last fun of the night after a roll like that, you dumb bitch, why the fuck did you do that?

"Come on, Coonan," Mickey said, rocking forward once from the effort it took to speak.

"Not yet, Grogan. I'm telling you, let that hand breathe for a while. Let it breathe and heal, and in a few weeks it might not look so much like a pile of bloody stool."

"That ain't right, you guys ain't right," Mickey said, shaking his head and dropping his gaze to the floor in a hopeless retreat, knowing the keep-away game wasn't as over as he thought it might be. "You guys ain't fair."

"*You guys ain't fair,*" Ape Drape whined. "Tell us a good nigger joke and maybe we'll give it back," he said.

Mickey slowly shook his head again.

"Pussy joke then," Joey Korosa finally uttered. "A good sloppy joke about gash," he said, the most drained-looking and sounding of them all.

And noticing this, and fearing he would soon get too tired to want to be with her alone, fearing he may have already forgotten about being alone with her just like he forgot about helping her find her relic, Suzy went to Joey from behind and touched his shoulder. She whispered, "There's nobody at the canal. I'm going there and I want you to go with me, and I want you to do it to me again on one of the benches down there." She was still drunk, and the words had come out much louder than she had intended.

"Oh boy, oh shit," Ape Drape said. "Get your ass down to that canal, Korosa. Go get your ass down there and go get your second set of rocks off."

Coonan lazily tossed and caught the bandage. "One nigger joke," he said. "One nigger joke and it's yours."

"I don't know no nigger jokes."

"Everybody knows nigger jokes, Grogan. Don't be such a lazy ass."

"Will you meet me there, Joey?" Suzy asked. "Will you come down to the canal?"

"Yes," he said. "I will come down to the canal. After this."

"After what?"

"This," he said, though he was feeling too wasted and tired and didn't think he had another load left in him yet to get his dick up and in her again. Maybe in a while if he put his mind to it. But there was Darly to consider. There was finding Darly to consider if she wasn't at home, and knowing her, she probably wasn't. She knew he'd eventually come looking, and would take off long before he even thought about it. And where to? He didn't want to think about where. He hated thinking about where, especially after their ugliest fights. Especially when he was wrong and he knew it and she knew it, and she'd take off for days and he hated thinking about where because he had his ideas about where. Those niggers. She was with those niggers. Those dudes she used to hang around with when she lived on that side of town. So he'd go looking for her and run himself nuts not finding her, run himself nuts in the strangled and irreversible liability of having been at fault for driving her to leave in the first place, a covetous and craving want to have her back in her bed all to himself, the great soft acres of that big dimpled ass, and the heavily bearded and salt-smelling cunt of hers all to himself, these fantasies then bringing on a maniacal nausea of regret that drilled his most recent memories of acting like such a mean and messed-up sonofabitch who had inside an evil snot of a kid who had to have the winning last word of every fight.

He'd take the 626 Cass Avenue bus over to Washington Street, Niggerville, and walk around the shitty little streets of it. The gated-up shops and the burned-out shops and the creepy nig graffiti sprayed everywhere, pitchforks and stars from the Vicelords and Disciples, the fat squiggled names like Spidey and Buddah and Roo-Roo. The jive-ass taverns he'd rush past, away from the flashy twangs of electric black guitar that spiked straight into his ears to liquefy his brains from where he came from, from where he was really supposed to be, white-ass motherfucker, and Christ, did that place scare the shit out of him. One small section of an entire galaxy in which he otherwise and literally feared nothing. To think that Darly might be somewhere deep within those places and with those people, kissing on them and drinking with them big meaty black bastards. Then, not finding her, all the way back on foot after the last bus route west had quit, well past midnight, a risky shortcut through the concrete parks and playgrounds between the drab, towering brick highrises that were the Will County Housing Authority's Robert Holmes Projects, marching through these spaces with his hands jammed deeply into his pockets, shaking, feeling followed, watched, and measured from the darkened door-ways and windows, finally returning empty-armed to Pulaski Street, chilly with sweat and tangled with an inward terror of loss and ravenous fantasy for the woman he had once again bullied away.

He told no one, not even Ape Drape or Coonan or Darly herself that he had gone to Washington Street looking for her, as he could never in his life admit that a girl, a girl for Chrissakes, a girl had made him so nuts. Nor could he explain to Ape Drape and Coonan why he had gone to that side of town for any goddamn reason, es-pecially for Darly. Not only because he wasn't her boyfriend, but because he didn't want them to know that he shared Darly's dugout with dark dick. They'd squint. Slap him upside the head. Ask him, What the fuck? What the hell you doing over there that time of night? Those nigs'll stick you for a nickel. Of course his friends knew about Darly and the blacks, and they'd never said any-thing to Joey about it. But Joey was often convinced that others were disgusted by knowing he balled Darly, and he sure as shit didn't want to talk about it.

And when she'd finally turn up, he wouldn't ask where she'd gone because then he would know, and knowing something for sure and having ideas about something were two totally different things. He knew they would fight again, fight badly, and he knew that after such fights she would split, and he had long ago decided that it was better to have ideas about where she was than to know for sure. Since in having an idea about where she was, roaming hunched and peering and half out of his head all over Niggerville for her, he would at least be able to rest the smallest portion of his worries on the chance that he might be wrong after all.

He knew he had to set things straight with Darly. He wanted to set things straight with her, and if she was already gone he'd grab the last eastbound bus to Washington Street and start roaming, no matter how fucked up and tired he felt. No, he wasn't her boy-friend. Joey Korosa wasn't anybody's goddamn boyfriend. But he had to set things straight with Darly, and that was that.

Because he could not stop thinking about the way her face looked in the busted window on the door he and Coonan had with all of their strength blocked to stop her from opening, her face then wicked and worthy of laughter. Red, round, spitting. The face of a crazed and furious whore slathered in come. Now the only way he could imagine her face was framed like a picture in the space where the black glass had been before she smashed the bottle through it, a framed picture on a dirty wall of someone suffering, a picture of someone he had hurt badly come right to moving life through some force that gave rage to the paper the picture was printed on, to spit and scream at him from the hour-old past, a picture that was branded, burning, in his hour-old memory, and one that he would never in his life want to laugh at.

Nor could he stop thinking about the way she had stripped and ambled through the tavern before they planted her at the end of the toilet daisy chain—though it really hadn't been unbearable, hearing her bucking and moaning like that, and here Joey's guilt quickly vacillated, since he had, after all, been tired as hell of Darly flipping out over the young piece he'd found earlier that night, the piece he'd eventually gotten to ball in the cooler. And besides, he'd tossed Darly away because she was being such a dumb goddamn pain in the ass, and goddamn her for the way she got in his face in front of everybody like that. And to look at who was begging him to take and nail her down by the canal, to take and nail her for the second time that night. Of course he could get it up again for a tight young piece like that. Goddamn right he could get his second set of rocks off. But what would he think about once he was done? Darly was what he would think about. Darly. And where. He hated to think about where.

Joey Korosa couldn't make up his mind. But he turned in his seat and glanced up at Suzy so he could look her in the eye and said, "Sure, I'll meet you down there. I will."

"Well hell," Ape Drape said, recognizing Joey's indecisive answer, "I'd a *gladly* taken Joey's place if he'd a said no. I'd a *gladly* taken his place," he said.

"Would you *please* give me back my bandage?" Mickey asked.

"No," Coonan answered, just as Suzy had stepped to the door to leave for the canal. "But *she* can have it!" Coonan said, and threw it to her. She caught the bandage in the doorway, caught it knowing this would end whatever was left of the keep-away game so that Joey would finally leave with her. And for a moment she waited for Joey to get up, but like the others, he just sat there watching Suzy with the bandage, wondering what she would do with it. She wondered what she would do with it as well.

Mickey Grogan pushed himself forward in a hobble, smiling, his good hand extended. "Here, please," he said. She would have handed it to him, but after two steps Ape Drape stuck his foot out and tripped Mickey, who collapsed again on his bad hand and howled. The room livened again with the same cruel laughter, and Mickey raised his eyes to Suzy, begging. She knew that one of them would just take the bandage, that the keep-away would start again, that Joey would never leave.

So Suzy held the bandage against her breast, and, running from the bar, she finally let the door slam behind her.

Good Friday crossed into the first hours of Holy Saturday, and the hard ugly sounds from the plant carried over the tiredly resigned community that neighbored it, as did the smoke that moved across a high and full moon. A shift whistle shrieked, and a freight train's brakes hissed somewhere close as it slowed in a way that reminded Suzy of herself.

She'd been waiting down by the canal for such a long time that she finally lay down on the bench she'd been sitting on, turning to look at the road that went uphill and crossed Pulaski Street at the corner where the Zimne Piwo Club sat, watching for Joey to come down. Aside from the canal, the smoke, the moon it crossed like a tattered curtain, no life moved anywhere. And though it was moist and stinking, she tucked the ball of bandage under her head, which ached and spun from the whole horrid night.

She jolted when she glanced up and saw someone jogging down the hill. She stood, and the pain in her head vanished. The body reached the bottom of the hill and called out her name, and she knew then that Joey Korosa would never come.

"Suzy!" the voice called.

And she was not afraid of Mickey Grogan, even though they were totally alone once again.

"Here, here," he said, gasping for breath. He held out his good hand to her once more. Hanging from it on a chain was her relic. "I found this," he said, huffing. "I saw Darly rip it off."

She took it without smiling and said, "Thanks."

"You seen my bandage?" Mickey asked. Suzy picked it up from the bench and handed it to him. For a second her fear returned, and she worried that her screams wouldn't reach past the gasping and clanging of the plant. But as she watched Mickey wince and quiver as he carefully wrapped up his hand, she knew that he wouldn't hurt her.

A barge was approaching, and when its horn roared over the water, both Suzy and Mickey jumped because the sound was so close, so enormous and loud. It was trolling quite close to the barge canal wall, so close that its wake sloshed against and over the wall and splashed on the gravel that shimmered like jewels in the moonlight, which was now uncovered since the wind had shifted south and drew the plant smoke to hover over a different direction.

"Goodbye, Suzy," Mickey said, and before she understood what he meant, Mickey hoisted himself onto the wall, then leapt into the barge as it passed. Suzy heard him grunt when he landed. He laughed as he floated away from Joliet. As he floated south forever.

Both Darly and Joey disappeared as well. She never again saw either of them on the bus, which she always rode alone, and she eventually stopped listening to the rumors about where they had gone whenever their names came up.

"They went and rescued Darly's nigger kids from the Holy Ghost Fathers Orphanage!" was the last thing Suzy heard; she couldn't stand listening to that garbage anymore. "Joey's a regular old nigger daddy!"

But in the early hours of that Holy Saturday, Suzy Kosasovich returned her relic around her neck and watched Mickey Grogan's barge troll away until the lights on the tugboat faded in the distance and the sound of its horn was only a timid echo of memory, and when it was gone she slowly made her way home, a quiet, dismal walk she tried to stall so that she wouldn't have to be alone in her bed with her thoughts, which, in those dark hours, dwelled on the terror of having to see Joey and Darly once Easter Vacation ended. Another beating. She imagined Darly kicking her in the stomach against the plastic seats on the bus down on the grimy rubber aisle. And Joey smirking and covering his mouth and making a crack to his friends who would whistle and laugh when Suzy climbed on board. But Joey and Darly would be gone for good when Easter Vacation ended, and Suzy rode the bus alone with the old women, and though the kids she rode with raised their crass racket, nobody bothered her.

Having drifted away from the moon, the plant smoke was a flat bleak weight in the sky. Suzy's drunkenness had eventually puddled down to a weak, defeated lucidity, shocked by the dimensions of cruelty she had not known before that night. People were mean, deep, and wicked, and she would never look at them, any of them, the same way again. And the strain of that truth made the walk home up the hill in the dark a heavy punishment. Another beating, Joey laughing a joke about screwing her in the cooler, Suzy never sensing in the slightest that she wouldn't see either of them again, and so completely unaware that Joey had left in his place a series of small roots that began then to tighten deep inside her body, a galaxy of spastic cells that twitched and divided and converged in the rapture of conception.

Winners of the Ruthanne Wiley Memorial Novella Contest

2006 *A Martyr for Suzy Kosasovich* by Patrick Michael Finn,
       selected by Tom Barbash

       A Momentary Jokebook by Jayson Iwen,
       selected by Tom Barbash

2005 *Isn't That Just Like You?* by Eric Anderson,
       selected by Michelle Herman
       (published with *Nothing and Two* by Ruthanne Wiley
       as *Duo Novellas, Volume 1*)

Other Recent Cleveland State University Poetry Center Titles

Nin Andrews. *The Book of Orgasms*
Dan Bellm. *Buried Treasure*
Christopher Burawa. *The Small Mystery of Lapses*
Jared Carter. *Les Barricades Mystérieuses*
John Donoghue. *A Small Asymmetry*
Diane Gilliam Fisher. *One of Everything*
Max Garland. *Hunger Wide as Heaven*
Douglas Goetsch. *The Job of Being Everybody*
Gaspar Pedro Gonzalez. *The Dry Season*
Susan Grimm, ed. *Ordering the Storm: How to Put Together
    a Book of Poems*
Linda Lee Harper. *Kiss, Kiss*
Sarah Kennedy. *Double Exposure*
Karen Kovacik. *Metropolis Burning*

George Looney. *Attendant Ghosts*
Alison Luterman. *The Largest Possible Life*
Helena Mesa. *Horse Dance Underwater*
Philip Metres. *To See the Earth*
Henri Michaux. *Someone Wants to Steal My Name*
Bern Mulvey. *The Fat Sheep Everyone Wants*
Deirdre O'Connor. *Before the Blue Hour*
Carol Potter. *Short History of Pets*
Barbara Presnell. *Piece Work*
Mary Quade. *Guide to Native Beasts*
Tim Seibles. *Buffalo Head Solos*
Tim Seibles. *Hammerlock*
Eliot Khalil Wilson. *The Saint of Letting Small Fish Go*
Sam Witt. *Sunflower Brother*
Margaret Young. *Willow from the Willow*